WEST FROM SINGAPORE

WEST FROM SINGAPORE

LOUIS L'AMOUR

BANTAM BOOKS

TORONTO • NEW YORK • LONDON • SYDNEY • AUCKLAND

WEST FROM SINGAPORE

*A Bantam Book / published by arrangement with
the author*

The Louis L'Amour Collection / July 1987

*If you would be interested in receiving bookends for
The Louis L'Amour Collection, please write to this address
for information:*

> *The Louis L'Amour Collection*
> *Bantam Books*
> *P.O. Box 956*
> *Hicksville, New York 11802*

ISBN 0-553-06306-5

Published simultaneously in the United States and Canada

---

*Bantam Books are published by Bantam Books, Inc. Its
trademark, consisting of the words "Bantam Books" and the
portrayal of a rooster, is Registered in U.S. Patent and Trademark Office and in other countries. Marca Registrada. Bantam
Books, Inc., 666 Fifth Avenue, New York, New York 10103.*

PRINTED IN THE UNITED STATES OF AMERICA

0 9 8 7 6 5 4 3 2 1

To Arlene Aizer, Stuart Applebaum, Diane Aronson, Barb Burg, Eileen Damore, Heather Florence, Renée Gelman, Sara Goodman, Linda Grey, Vicky Heredia, Kevin Jones, Stan Last, Yook Louie, Nick Mazzella, Serafina Messina, Michael Morrison, Jim Plumeri, David Ruitenberg, Sandy Su, Beverly Susswein and Alberto Vitale for support above and beyond the call.

CONTENTS

FOREWORD

The stories in this collection and in a previous one, Night Over the Solomons, were written either just before World War II or after it had begun. It was not easy for a writer to get started then, and it is not easy now. The stories were a desperate effort to keep eating while working on a novel that, as a result of my going into the Army, was never completed.

During those early years I planned to write stories of the sea. The Pacific islands fascinated me, as did the coasts of Southeast Asia. Every island had its story. Already I had learned that a writer, if he expects to write much, must observe and remember. Often there is no chance to return and look again, even if the place remains unchanged, which is rare indeed.

To observe and remember—these things were important— but it was also important to listen well. The islands and seas of which I write were filled with color and excitement. It was easy to be carried away with all of that and to forget what was necessary. There were stories of shipwreck and mutiny, of blackbirding and pearl diving, of piracy and treasure. Captain Bligh had brought his open boat through these waters after the mutiny on the *Bounty*. La Pérouse had vanished somewhere down here. Magellan had been killed here after what Europeans consider the first crossing of the Pacific. But there were a thousand and one stories of only locally known people who had met the sea and the islands and survived.

Although I am considered a western writer, and although I grew up in the west, my first stories were these, of the islands of Indonesia and neighboring waters. Wandering from port to port I met adventurers, planters, gold and diamond seekers and pearl buyers, men who sought the far places of the earth for one reason or another, just as I was doing. They were not unlike men I had known in mining camps and on cow ranches in the American west. Yet their motivations were different, for western men came to build and to create, not just to get rich and get out. Only in the goldfields of California could one find the counterparts to the drifters out for the main chance I came to know in the Pacific.

The hero of the stories in this book is Ponga Jim Mayo, a sailor of fortune who was the master of the *Semiramis*, a tramp freighter he would sail up and down the waters of the Pacific islands in search of a living. He was an Irish-American who had served his first years at sea sailing out of Liverpool and along the west coast of Africa's Ponga River, where he picked up his nickname.

He's a character I created from having gotten to know men just like him while I was a seaman in my yondering days. I sailed on a variety of steamers, freighters, and schooners back then, but I didn't stay on any one for too long. I would sail from one port to another, drop one ship and pick up another to go on someplace else. One time I went to sea from Los Angeles and took a trip completely around the world, ending up in New York. From there I took a tanker and went around to the west coast of the Panama Canal. On my first long trip, I served as an ordinary seaman. By my third trip I had passed the examination to become an able-bodied seaman, or A.B., as one is called. For a while I shipped on a schooner as a second mate where part of my job was to keep track of everything bought and sold for a captain who was very bright but who could read and write only with difficulty.

The ships on which I sailed around the East Indian islands got into all kinds of small ports to which no steamships or freighters ever sailed. We had an outboard motor on a launch that enabled us to go to a lot of remote places to pick up cargo where the tramp freighters couldn't reach. So I was able to visit places other men only dreamed of knowing.

The master of a tramp freighter in Far Eastern waters, like Ponga Jim Mayo, had to have a wide range of experience and information to succeed, and connections were extremely important. Knowing who had something to ship, knowing the availability of seasonal cargoes and the people who delegated the shipments, could make business easier and success more certain. Much of this is handled by the ship's owners or their agents, but local knowledge was always important.

Much smaller, lighter cargo was handled by native-owned vessels, mostly sailing craft. Anticipating the outbreak of war, both the Japanese and Germans had established undercover relationships in the islands, to prepare for invasion in the case of the Japanese and in cooperation with merchant raiders in the case of the Germans.

There were always dissident elements, and even more common were those who looked merely for profit, not caring who it hurt if they made a fat dollar.

Ponga Jim Mayo was simply a ship's master who fell into the path of history while just trying to make a living. Necessity as well as personal loyalties brought him into conflict with those who were preparing the way for invasion.

No other area on earth offers so many islands, so many small coves, harbors, and lagoons, so many rivers opening to the sea, and so great a variety of population, but to a seafaring man accustomed to those waters any vessel operating out of the normal pattern would arouse curiosity and, at such a time, suspicion.

There are few secrets in such areas. Shipping men are known to each other, and there is much rumor and gossip around the waterfront bars as well as in those more elaborate clubs further back from the sea. Nothing much happened that somebody did not know about, and such a man as Ponga Jim would have picked up all the scuttlebutt from along the waterfronts. Soerbaia, Samarang, Medan, Amurang, Makassar, Balikpapan, Port Moresby, Hollandia, and such places always had a few people who knew what was happening or about to happen.

Ponga Jim would have been familiar to all these people and would over the years have formed friendships or business relationships in all these places, including Darwin and Broome on the north coast of Australia.

The setting for Ponga Jim's adventures, Indonesia, known before World War II as the East Indies, is without a doubt one of the most fascinating localities on earth. It consists of some 13,000 islanders scattered along the equator with a total land area of 735,268 square miles. In those years it was referred to as the Netherlands East Indies, and the administration was Dutch. The British had interests there also, but ships came from all over the world, picking up or delivering cargo. Only the K.P.M. boats, a Dutch line, worked the smaller ports. Otherwise the shipping was native craft, mostly under sail, often with auxiliary motors.

Long before the coming of European traders, ancient civilizations were here, and ships came often from India, Arabia, and China. A thousand years before Columbus sailed to America, ships had left the Sunda Strait (between Java and Sumatra) to sail the 3,300 miles to Madagascar, a voyage considerably longer.

Of this I knew nothing when I arrived. It was during my knockabout years, and I was taking jobs where and when they could be found, at sea or ashore. Nothing in my schooling had prepared me for what I was to discover.

On a day away from my ship I hired an Arab boy to sail me over to a nearby island where I wanted to see a ruin that looked interesting. As he spoke English quite well, I asked how long he had been in the islands. He told me his people had been there for nearly four hundred years!

A missionary to whom I spoke knew less than I. When I asked him about the boy's statement, he shrugged it off with the comment that one heard all sorts of stories. About 170 languages are spoken in Indonesia, but Malay was the tongue of the marketplace, and English speakers were not hard to find. Oddly enough, it was from that trading schooner captain who could barely read and write that I learned something of what I needed to know.

Although uneducated in the usual sense, he was an intelligent man who had spent fifty years in the islands. His curiosity had been aroused by ancient ruins, and he asked questions. Years of trading had built him a strong relationship with many of the peoples of the the islands, and they talked as freely to him as among themselves. It was from him that I first heard of the extensive trade with India, China, and the Arabs beginning we do not know when but certainly flourishing in the first century after Christ.

Gradually, I traced the story of the great island empires of

Shrivijaya and Shailendra, to name but two. The earliest positive date for Chinese knowledge of Bali is A.D. 977, but Hindu culture had already established itself by A.D. 400 Ptolemy, the geographer from Alexandria, refers to these islands as early as A.D. 160 Fa-Hien, the Chinese pilgrim, was in the islands in A.D. 414.

Celebes, now called Sulawesi, is a large island in Indonesia (formerly the East Indies), lying just east of Borneo. It is about 550 miles long, with an area of 71,400 square miles. Four long arms extend from the central body of the island. The northern peninsula runs out into the sea for some 400 miles and is nowhere more than 60 miles wide.

Forty years ago, at the time of these stories, Celebes was ruled by the Netherlands. The people fell roughly into two groups, the Muslims and the pagans, largely animists. The largest groups were the Bugis (exceptional seamen), the Manders, the Makassars, and a more primitive people, the Toradjas.

Rivers are short, and a series of mountain ranges run largely north and south through the central part of the island. Mountains extend the full 400 miles of the northern peninsula. Gorontalo, a town of approximately 6,000 people, was located on the south side of the northern peninsula and was served three times a week by K.P.M. steamers. Various native craft came and went, and occasionally British Blue Funnel boats would call.

The climate is hot and subject to tropical rains. The products were largely wax, skins, tortoise shell, and forest products. Europeans were predominantly Dutch, with a few Englishmen and the usual scattering of other nationalities. Around the waterfronts of this and other such ports are usually a few drifters, vagabonds of the islands, of various or mixed nationality.

It's been fun for me to go back over these stories in preparing this book for publication. The world may have changed a good deal since I first wrote them, but a lot of those ports where the stories took place haven't changed a bit. And I'll be glad if they never change much.

AUTHOR'S NOTE

GORONTALO

The river is deep and the anchorage not very good. At the time of the story the town of Gorontalo had a population of about six thousand—a picturesque little port on the south side of a long peninsula. As in most of these small ports there was, aside from the local people, a certain number of drifters, adventurers, treasure hunters, ship's officers out of a job, and men tramping the island for one reason or another, most of them hoping to pick up an odd dollar here or there.

John Russell has written well of these islands, and so has Somerset Maugham.

EAST OF GORONTALO

Ponga Jim Mayo leaned against the hogshead of tobacco and stared out at the freighter. His faded khaki suit was rumpled, his heavy jaw unshaven. The white-topped cap carried the label "Captain" in gold lettering, but Ponga Jim looked like anything but a master mariner, and felt even less like one.

Being broke was a problem anywhere. In Gorontalo it became an emergency of the first water. Everything he owned in the world was on him, from the soft, woven-leather shoes on his feet to the white-topped cap to the big Colt automatic in its shoulder holster.

Jim pushed his cap back on his head and glanced at Major Arnold, sitting on a bitt at the edge of the wharf. In his neat white drill and military mustache he could have been nothing but a British officer.

"Tell me, William," Jim said, "just what brings a big-shot intelligence officer to Celebes? Something in the wind?"

"You get around a lot, don't you?" Major William Arnold lighted a cigarette and glanced up at Jim.

"Yeah, when I can." Ponga Jim grinned. "Right now I'm on the beach, and it looks like I'm not getting off for a while. But there isn't much in the Indies I don't know."

Arnold nodded. "I know. You might do me some good, Jim. If you see anything suspicious, give me a tip, will you? There's a rumor around that while England's busy in Europe, there

3

will be a move to pick up some of her colonies in the Far East. This is a Dutch colony, but we're cooperating."

"Then," Mayo said thoughtfully, nodding his head toward the broad-beamed, battered tramp freighter, "you might add her to your list of suspects."

"That's the *Natuna* out of Surabaya, isn't it? Didn't you used to be her skipper?"

"Yeah." Ponga Jim shifted his position to let the breeze blow under his coat. He was wearing a gun, and the day was hot. "Then the company sold her to Pete Lucieno, and I quit. I wouldn't work for that dope peddler on a bet. I'm no lily of the valley, and frankly, I'm not making any boasts about being above picking up a slightly illegal dollar—I've made some of your British pearl fisheries out of season before now, and a few other things—but I draw the line at Pete's kind of stuff."

"No love lost, I guess?" Arnold squinted up at Jim, smiling.

"Not a bit. He'd consider it a privilege to cut my heart out. So would Dago Frank, that major-domo of his, or Blue Coley. And I don't fancy them."

Major Arnold soon left, walking back up toward the club. Ponga Jim lighted a cigarette and stared thoughtfully at the *Natuna*. Then his eyes shifted to the other ship in port, a big white freighter, the *Carlsberg*. Although there were three or four schooners, and a scattering of smaller craft, it was the two freighters that held his attention.

"Now, Major William," he said whimsically, "you should never miss a bet. Being an old seafaring man, it strikes me as being somewhat phony for that native scow to be shoving herself around in circles. Especially when she goes behind the *Carlsberg* riding high and comes out with darn little freeboard. Then she wanders around, gets behind the *Natuna*, and comes out riding high in the water again.

"Now the only *Carlsberg* I ever knew sailed out of Bremen, not Copenhagen." Mayo's eyes flickered to the sleek white *Carlsberg*. "So, putting together a possibility of registry changed from Bremen to Copenhagen, some mysterious goings-on connected with the *Natuna*, a scow whose owners would frame their mothers for a dollar six-bits, a war, and William's rumors, what do you have?"

Ponga Jim Mayo straightened up and sauntered off down the dock. It was nearly sundown, and the seven guilders that remained in his pocket suggested food. After that—

Jim walked into Chino John's and stopped at the bar.

"Give me a beer," he said, glancing around. A man standing nearby turned to face Mayo.

"Well, if it isn't my old friend Ponga Jim!" he sneered. "On the beach again, no?"

Jim looked at Dago Frank coolly and then past him at Lucieno. The fat little Portuguese glistened with perspiration and ill-concealed hatred.

"Yeah," Jim said. "Anytime to keep out of the company of rats."

"I disdain that remark," Lucieno said. "I disdain it."

"You'd better," Jim said cheerfully. "If you took it up, I'd pull your fat nose for you!"

Dago Frank's eyes narrowed. He stepped closer.

"Then maybe you pull mine, eh?" he challenged.

Ponga Jim's right fist snapped up in a jarring right that knocked every bit of wind from Dago Frank's body. Then Jim jerked him across his knee. Unsnapping his belt with a deft twist of the fingers, he jerked down Dago's trousers, and while the raging man gasped for breath, proceeded to whip him soundly!

Then, jerking him erect, Mayo jolted another six-inch punch into his midsection and dropped him to the floor. Coolly, he picked up his beer and drank it, and then he turned and looked at Lucieno. The fat Portuguese began to back away, his face white.

Jim grinned. "Okay, pal," he said cheerfully. "It was just a little lesson to teach your boyfriend to talk nice to his superiors. Next time—" He shook his finger warningly and turned away.

Arnold was standing on the boardwalk as Jim strode through the swinging doors. He chuckled, clapping Jim on the shoulder.

"That was great! Everybody in the Dutch East Indies has been hoping to see that pair get called. But you've made an enemy, and a nasty one."

"That's just the fifth episode," Mayo said, shrugging. "I beat them out of a cargo of copra and pearl shell down in the Friendly Islands about three years ago. About six months later they tried to kidnap old Schumann's daughter over in the Moluccas. They were going to sell her to some native prince. I put a stop to that, and a couple of their boys got tough."

"What happened to them?"

"You know, William," Jim said seriously, "I was trying to remember the other day. They had an accident or something."

He straightened his tie, and gave the automatic a hitch into a better position.

"By the way, William," he asked carelessly, "where's the *Natuna* bound this trip?"

"To Port Moresby, with general cargo."

Ponga Jim walked down the street, and when he turned at the corner, glanced back. Major Arnold, his neat, broad-shouldered, compact figure very casual, was standing in front of Chino John's. Jim grinned, and turned the corner carelessly. Then, suddenly alert, he wheeled and darted down an alley, turned into a side street, and cut through the scattering of buildings toward the dock. The British Intelligence was convenient at times, at others, a nuisance.

There was no one in sight when he reached the dock. He let himself down the piling and crawled into a skiff moored there in the dark. Quickly, he shoved off.

Overhead there was a heavy bank of clouds. The night was very still, and the skiff made scarcely a shadow as it slipped through the dark water. Staying a hundred yards off, Ponga Jim avoided the lighted gangway and cautiously sculled the boat around to the dark side of the *Natuna*. There was no one in sight, so with painstaking care he drifted the boat nearer and nearer to the silent ship. When he came alongside he laid his paddle down and stood up, balancing himself.

Fortunately, the sea was still. Picking up the heaving line lying in the stern of the boat, Mayo tossed the monkey's fist around a stanchion of the taffrail, and catching the ball, he pulled it down.

Once aboard that ship he would be practically in the hands of his enemies and with no legal status. Ponga Jim grinned and settled the gun in its holster. Then, taking two strands of the heaving line, he climbed swiftly—hand over hand.

There was no one in sight, and, pulling himself through the rail, he rolled over twice and was against the bulkhead of the after wheelhouse. There was no movement aft. Forward, the light from a port glinted on the rail and the water, and he could see the watchman standing under the light near the gangway. It was Blue Coley.

Jim crawled into the shadow of the winch and then along the deck to the ladder. The well deck was empty, so he slipped down. Then he hesitated.

The passage was lighted, but it was a chance he had to take. The crew's quarters were forward, the officers' amidships. There was small chance of anyone being aft. He stepped into the passageway and hurried along, passing the paint locker. The rope-locker door was fastened, and he swore as he dug for his keys. Luckily, he still had them. Once inside, he closed the door carefully and locked it again.

There was a stifling smell of paint and linseed oil. He felt his way along over coils of line, until he stopped abruptly. Then, cautiously, he struck a match. The paint had been shifted into the rope locker. Carefully, he snuffed the match and then paused in indecision. Then he crawled over the coils of line and found the door into number five hatch. He grinned. Luckily, he knew every inch of the *Natuna*. He hadn't commanded her for a year for nothing, and he liked to know a ship. He knew her better now than the man who built her. She'd changed a lot in twenty years, and there had been repairs made and some changes.

The door was stiff, but he opened it and crawled into the hold, carefully closing the door after him. He was on his hands and knees on a wooden case.

He struck a match, shielding it with his hands despite the knowledge that the hold was sealed tight and the hatch battened down and ready for the sea. The case was marked in large black letters, CANNED GOODS. Returning to the rope locker, Jim picked up a marlinespike and returned to the hold. Working carefully, he forced open the wooden case. Striking another match, he leaned over.

Then he sat back on his heels, smiling. The case was filled with automatic rifles.

"Well, well, Señor Lucieno!" he muttered to himself. "Just as I suspected. If there's dirty work, you'll be in on it."

Thoughtfully, he considered the open case. The match had gone out, but he could remember those cool barrels, the magazines. He rubbed his jaw.

"Contraband," he said. "And I'm broke. What was it Hadji Ali used to say? 'Lie to a liar, for lies are his coin; steal from a thief, for that is easy; lay a trap for the trickster, and catch him at the first attempt; but beware of an honest man.' "

Taking one of the rifles from the case he began to assemble it in the dark.

"Well, Petey, old darling, you're a liar, a thief, and a trickster, and contraband is fair game for anyone—so here's where I move in."

Fastening the case shut, he carried the automatic rifle with him. Then he descended into the lower hold, and found a place near the shaft-alley housing where there was a space in the cargo. He had known it was there. Stowing cargo in that spot always necessitated it because of the ship's structure. There was also a small steel door into the shaft alley. So far as he knew it had not been used since he had ordered it cut there while making repairs. Opening another case he got some excelsior and made himself comfortable. Then, crawling back into the 'tween decks, he felt his way over the cases until he was immediately under the hatch.

Listening, he heard no feet on the deck, so he opened a case. As he had suspected, this was really canned goods. He tried several cases, and with his coat for a sack, carried an armful back down to his hideout.

"If you're going to stow away, Jim boy," he told himself, "by all means pick a ship you know, and one carrying food."

Opening a can of pineapple he ate, speculating on the future. The *Natuna* was bound for Port Moresby. That would mean something like ten or twelve days. It might be more, depending on the weather. The *Natuna* was a temperamental old Barnacle Bill of a ship. She might stagger along at twelve knots, and she might limp at eight or nine. It was hot, too damned hot, but during at least part of the day he could stay in the 'tween decks under a ventilator.

Besides, there wasn't a chance of his being here ten days. Pete Lucieno wasn't one to spend a dime or a guilder he could save, and that would mean he wouldn't take this cargo a bit farther than he could help. If he was bound for Port Moresby, that meant he was discharging the contraband somewhere this side of there, and if he was going that far, it meant his point of discharge wouldn't be very much this side. Which meant that he was heading somewhere along the New Guinea coast, and probably the mouth of the Fly. There were islands there and easy access to the interior.

Obviously, whoever planned to use these rifles and the other munitions, intended to distribute them among the natives and then stir up trouble. By raiding Port Moresby, friction could be created and the entire Indies might be set aflame. Then it would require British action to protect her nationals and save her colonies.

*   *   *

During the next two nights, Ponga Jim Mayo searched the paint locker and the lamp locker. As he had suspected, both were stored with ammunition. He picked up some for the automatic rifle, and found some clips for his automatic, stuffing his pockets with them.

For water, he had to go to the gravity tank on the boat deck. Otherwise his only chance was to enter the crew's quarters forward or the galley or mess room amidships. Neither was practical. As for the boat deck, by crawling through the bulkhead door into number four and then into number three hatch, he could climb the ladder to the 'tween decks and from the top of the cargo, could scramble into the ventilator just abaft the cargo winches at number three hatch. From the ventilator cowl he had a good view of the deck without being seen, and it was simple to slip out and up the ladder to the boat deck.

On the fifth night, Mayo slipped out of the ventilator and walked across the deserted deck to the ladder, climbing to the boat deck. He drank, and then filled the can he'd carried with him.

Crouching near the tank, he could see the officer on watch pacing the bridge. By his thick shoulders and queer gait, Jim recognized him as Blue Coley. That would mean, he reflected, that Dago Frank would have the eight-to-twelve watch. Lucieno couldn't navigate and knew nothing of seamanship, so obviously someone else had the eight to four. Ponga Jim wrinkled his brow thoughtfully. Now who the devil?

Long ago he had discovered it was well to know the caliber of one's opponent. Dago Frank was a vindictive, treacherous, blood-hungry rascal who would stop at nothing. Blue Coley was a thick-headed strong-armed thug without enough on the ball to carry through a job of this kind.

Suddenly Jim flattened out on the deck. Aft, near the ventilator he used for access to the deck, was a slight, square-shouldered figure. Even as he watched, the man came forward soundlessly, and as he moved across the ribbon of light from the starboard passage, he was clearly revealed for an instant. He was a lascar in dark green cotton trousers which flapped about his legs halfway between knee and ankle, and his head was done up in a red turban. There was a puckering scar on the man's face, and he was muscular. In his belt was an ugly-looking kris.

Now what's this? Jim felt himself getting irritated. Had the fellow seen him? And who was he? How did he figure in this deal? If one of the crew, he had no reason to be ducking or dodging around. Unless, that is, he was aft when he had no business to be.

Watching, Jim saw the native come forward stealthily and then suddenly dodge out of sight near the starboard rail. There was a walk forward along the rail outside the amidships house.

But scarcely had he disappeared when a shadow appeared in the lighted passage, and then a man walked out on deck. Jim's eyes narrowed.

It was a heavy, brutal head set down on massive shoulders with scarcely any neck at all. The shoulders were enormously wide and thick, the chest was deep, and when he walked his knees jerked queerly, like those of some wrestlers. When he turned, Jim could see a flattened nose above a mouth like a gash set in a wide, dark face. It was a face marked with brutality and strength, and the whole man radiated a sense of evil power that Ponga Jim had never seen in any other human thing.

When he lifted his hands, Jim could see they were thick and powerful with stubby fingers and backed by huge-boned wrists. A black beard darkened the man's jaw, and there was a mat of hair visible at his open shirt. Despite the brutality in the man's face, there was a shrewd sort of animal cunning, too.

Ponga Jim Mayo felt the hair prickle along the back of his neck, and he wet his lips thoughtfully. Without doubt this was the skipper, and he was something far different from Dago Frank or Blue Coley. When the man went back into the passage, Jim slipped down the ladder and aft to his ventilator, but he was no sooner inside than he heard footsteps approaching.

11

He hesitated, gun in hand. His jaw set hard. If they found him now, there would be nothing to do but shoot it out.

Two men stopped near the ventilator. Lucieno was speaking.

"We're making good time. The day after tomorrow we will drop the anchor in the mouth of the Fly. Gruber will be there to meet us."

"What about Borg?" Dago's voice was cautious.

"We let Borg alone," Lucieno said severely, "if we know what is good for us." He hesitated. "You know what he thinks? He thinks somebody's aboard—a stowaway."

Jim felt his heart pounding, and his mouth went dry.

"A stowaway?" Dago Frank broke in. "That is not possible, unless—"

"Jim Mayo, you think, eh? I think, too. Borg, he think he see somebody on the main deck. Two nights ago. The night we leave Gorontalo, he see an empty boat floating. Now somebody been in the chart room. He say that."

"What now?" Dago Frank asked. "I like to get hold of him, of that Ponga Jim."

The two walked off forward, and Jim slipped down into the 'tween decks and then down the ladder to his hideout. Once there, he checked the automatic and, returning it to its holster, checked the automatic rifle. Then he pulled a case over the opening and stretched out.

It could only have been a few minutes when he was awakened suddenly. Every sense alert, he waited, listening. There was silence, then the scratching of a match. In the dim light thrown against the bulkhead he could see a shadow. It looked like a lascar turban, but he couldn't be sure. The gun slid into his hand, and crouching, breathless, he awaited discovery. None came.

There were soft movements and then a metallic sound, a short hard blow, and then another. And silence. He waited a long time, but there was no further movement. Crawling out of his concealment, he felt his way over the cases. In the top tier, a case of canned goods had been pulled aside. He knew every case from crawling over them so much. A faint scent of oil came to his nostrils and, shielding it carefully, he struck a match.

The end of one of the boards in the case had been saturated with oil and then forced open bit by bit, and more oil added, effectively quieting any possible screech from a nail!

But who? Ponga Jim returned to his hideout distinctly uneasy. He had a feeling that matters were getting out of hand: the unknown skipper, obviously a more dangerous and cunning man than either Frank or Lucieno, and now this mysterious searcher. Added to that was the problem of the lascar. Still puzzling over the problem, he fell asleep.

He awakened with a start, instantly conscious of two things. He had overslept, and something was definitely wrong. Crawling to his knees he slipped on his shoulder holster and then his coat. Putting on his cap, he waited, listening.

There was no sound. But suddenly he was conscious of a peculiar odor. He frowned, trying to place it. Then it struck him like a blow!

Formaldehyde! Evidently, while he slept too soundly, they had crept through the hold or at least looked in.

Not seeing him and fearing to stumble across an armed man, they were trying to smoke him out.

Lunging to his feet, he hurriedly shifted the case over the entrance to his hideout. By that time the fumes were growing thick. Stumbling over the cargo, he found the door into number four.

His heart sank. The door was locked tight. Wheeling about, gasping and choking, he stumbled across to the rope-locker door. It, too, was locked. For an instant he hesitated, his mind desperately searching for a way out. Then he remembered the plate into the shaft alley. Stumbling back over the cargo, he tumbled into his hole and pulled the case back over the entrance; then he turned and felt for the plate. Finding it, he found the wrench he had thoughtfully stolen from the locker and started on one of the nuts.

13

It was stiff, rusty. Desperately, he tugged. The wrench came loose, and he skinned his knuckles on the nut below. Choking, eyes red and breath coming in gasps, he got one of the nuts loose and then another. He thought the final nut would never come off. Twice the wrench slipped loose. Then suddenly it was off, and he slid through the hole into the darkness of the shaft alley.

Coughing and spluttering, he struck a match. The great whirling metallic shaft loomed above him. He dropped the match, and taking the plate by a bolt through its center, he slipped it back on the bolts. Turning, he walked forward to the swing door, moving carefully. Beyond it, the shaft alley was lighted. Running now, he slipped the Colt from its holster. Amazingly enough, the shaft-alley door was open, and even as he plunged through and closed it after him, he was conscious of the bad seamanship. Now if he were still in command—

The engineer on watch didn't even look up, and the fireman was arguing with the oiler in the fire room. Crossing the floor plates in two jumps, Ponga Jim ran up the ladder to the orlop deck, then forward to the ladder to the main deck. Just as he reached it, a lascar came down the ladder, and his eyes went wide when he saw Mayo. Jerking up the spanner he carried, the lascar tried to strike, but Jim stiff-armed him with a left and knocked the native sprawling.

It was quiet on deck, and the sun was shining when Mayo stepped out of the passage. He realized then that he had overslept by many hours, for it was already late in the afternoon. Off on the port side was the long blue line of the New Guinea coast, and he stood there, letting his eyes grow accustomed to the sun. Aft, he could hear voices.

Then he started forward and ran up the ladder to the bridge.

As he stepped into the wheelhouse the lascar at the wheel gave a sharp cry. Dago Frank, evidently on watch while the skipper tried to smoke out the stowaway, wheeled. His face turned gray, and he grabbed at a gun. Then Ponga Jim slugged him.

14

Frank toppled forward, his jaw slack, and Jim slugged him again. Then he turned on the man at the wheel.

"Put her over to port about ten degrees," he snapped. "Quick now, or I'll spill your guts on this deck!"

His face white with fear, the lascar put the wheel over. A sudden sound from the chart room startled Jim, and he whirled to see Pete Lucieno standing in the door, pistol in hand.

"Drop it!" Mayo snapped.

Lucieno smiled—and dropped the gun. Then he bowed slightly.

"Of course, my friend. With the greatest of pleasure. I see you now where I have long wished to see you."

"Wha—?"

Then something crashed down on the back of his head, and a sharp arrow of pain stabbed through his consciousness as he felt himself falling.

When Ponga Jim Mayo opened his eyes, his head was throbbing with pain. He tried to move, and surprisingly, he was not bound. He sat up, groaning.

"Comin' out of it?"

He looked up, blinking back the pain. Borg, his powerful legs braced to the roll of the ship, stood looking down at him. The man had a pair of field glasses in his right hand. He shifted them to his left.

"Get up."

Ponga Jim crawled unsteadily to his feet, facing Borg. The man stared at him.

"Ponga Jim Mayo, eh? Tough guy, are you?" He swung. His fist smashed against the angle of Jim's jaw, and Mayo went down. He got up, staggering, and Borg hit him again.

Then Borg laughed. "You may be tough around this bunch of punks, but you ain't tough t' me, see?"

He walked over to Jim and kicked him viciously in the ribs. Jim started to get up, and, sneering, Borg swung a vicious kick

15

at his head. Mayo rolled over and swung his ankle up behind Borg's leg, spilling the big man to the deck.

With a snarling oath, Borg scrambled to his feet, his face livid. He swung a terrific right, but Jim ducked and hooked a left to the body. Even as he threw it, he knew he didn't have the stuff. The punch landed, and then Jim hooked his right to Borg's head, but the man grabbed him and hurled him across the room.

Following him, Borg slammed a wicked right to the head that made Ponga Jim roll and grab at the shelf along the wall. Then Borg hooked him in the kidney and dug a wicked right into his body. As Jim started to fall, he felt a terrific blow crash against his jaw.

It seemed hours later when he came to. He kept his eyes shut and lay very still, conscious that he was bound hand and foot now, and conscious that there were two men in the chart room, one at the wheel.

Opening his eyes to a slit, Jim saw the man at the wheel was a lascar, but not the one who had been there when he was fighting Borg. The two men came out of the chart room, and he saw one was Dago Frank, the other Lucieno.

"In about an hour he say, " Lucieno said. "The submarine he come in about an hour."

"This one," Frank said, motioning toward Mayo, "I like to kill."

The two went out on the bridge, and Jim lay very still, resting, his desperate thoughts striving through the stabbing pain to find a way out. He stretched a little, but the ropes were tight. Borg was a seaman, and Borg had tied those ropes to stay.

Jim lay still, staring through his half-opened eyes at the helmsman's feet. Suddenly, his eyes lifted—green flapping trousers, a wide leather belt, an ugly kris, and then broad, muscular brown shoulders and a dark red turban. It was the lascar

16

who had been prowling that night on deck! And the one, he felt sure, who had opened a box of rifles in number five hold.

There was something phony about this somewhere. He lay still, feigning unconsciousness. Another lascar came in, relieving the man at the wheel. Ponga Jim heard the course as they repeated it, and he started.

In the excitement, the lascars had continued to steer his course, ten degrees north and east of the proper one! He stirred a little, to get a better view of the room. Then in a far corner, among some signal flags, he glimpsed his gun! Evidently flying from his hand when he was struck from behind, it had fallen among those flags, unnoticed.

In an hour, Lucieno had said. At least fifteen minutes had passed, possibly more. He lifted his eyes. They stopped, riveted on a bit of red outside the starboard door of the wheelhouse. The lascar was standing on the ladder, concealed unless the man at the wheel noticed him, or unless Dago Frank walked along the bridge. The red turban came into sight and then the scar-puckered face.

The man at the wheel was daydreaming, staring off at the coastline to port. The lascar at the door lifted a knife into view, laid it carefully on the deck, and shot it slithering straight at Jim. Instinctively, he arched his body. The man at the wheel jerked around, staring.

The knife was safely under Jim's body, and the lascar in the doorway was gone. Outside the door an awning string rattled against the stanchion. The lascar peered, started to call to Frank, and then shrugged and was silent. Working carefully, Jim got the knife turned edgewise. It was razor sharp. Holding himself carefully, so as not to slice off a finger, he managed to use his hands enough to cut through a rope and then another. Swiftly, he freed himself and stood up.

The lascar turned, and found himself with a knife pressed against his stomach. His face gray, he stood very still, his mouth looking sick.

"One sound and I'll cut your heart out!" Jim snapped. "Get back to that wheel, and don't let a yelp out of you!"

17

Turning, he caught up the automatic and stepped to the door. Dago Frank was standing in the wing of the bridge, staring at the shoreline. It was suddenly very near, too near. He wheeled and started for the wheelhouse, and brought up suddenly.

"All right, Dago," Jim said coolly, "this is it. You wanted to kill me, now go for your gun!"

Frank's hand shot down, and Ponga Jim stood very still, canting to the roll of the ship. When Dago Frank's gun came up belching flame, he fired. He heard a bullet smack viciously into the wall of the wheelhouse, but that was all. Frank turned half around and fell headlong.

A white man rushed out on deck with a rifle, and Ponga Jim fired. The man ran three steps and then pitched headlong over the rail, the rifle clattering on the deck. Blue Coley started out of the passageway below, and Jim's gun coughed. The bullet smacked against a steam-pipe housing at his feet, and Blue stumbled back into the passage in a desperate hurry. Another shot chased him down the passage.

Leaping through the door, Jim was just in time to snap a shot at the lascar at the wheel as the man tried to throw a knife. The native dropped, coughing blood. Jim leaped past him to the engine-room telegraph and jerked it over to SLOW—then to STOP.

A bullet whistled by his head and smashed the chronometer, and he saw an oiler standing in the forecastle door. Jim fired, and the man jumped back inside. Another rifle shot crashed, and then Ponga Jim chanced a shot into the open doorway, and there was nothing further. He turned suddenly, snapping a shot at a gun in a forecastle port.

Borg had come up the other ladder and was standing in the doorway, staring at him. The man was unshaven, and his face was almost black.

Ponga Jim glanced down at the empty automatic, tossed it aside.

"I got something for you, big boy," he said. His left jabbed quickly, but Borg ducked and laughed, crashing right into a whipping right uppercut.

"Go ahead, Jim!" a voice shouted from the door behind him. "I'll hold this bunch!"

Mayo whirled, stepping back to watch the door and Borg at the same time. The lascar with the red turban stood in the doorway with an automatic rifle. He was grinning.

"William!" Ponga Jim shouted. "William, by all that's holy!"

"Righto, old chap!"

The cheery voice sounded in his ears as Borg rushed. Jim lashed out with another left, and this time stabbed Borg over the eye, splitting it to the bone. A ponderous fist crashed against the side of Jim's head, and a million stars sprang into the sky. Jim laughed suddenly, full of the lust to fight, and fired both hands into the big man's body furiously.

Borg hooked a hard left to his head and then grabbed him, but Ponga Jim jerked away, crossing a short right to the face, and hooking a left to the body. Borg rushed, clubbing with his right, but missing. Then suddenly Borg launched himself in a vicious flying tackle!

Ponga Jim's knee jerked up into the man's face, knocking him sprawling to the deck. But Borg was up, a wild right catching Jim in the body. He gasped, and a left slammed against his head, dropping him to his knees. Borg lunged, kicking, and Ponga Jim hurled himself at the one leg Borg had on the floor.

The big man came down with a crash, and then both men were on their feet. Jim walked in wide open, his eyes blazing with the joy of battle. Left-right, left-right, punch after punch he ripped into the big man's head and body, hooks, uppercuts, and swings, a battering volley.

Borg was powerful, but too slow. He started to back up, lifting his arms to get that blinding fury of punches out of his eyes and face only to catch a terrific right in the solar plexus. He gasped and Jim let him have another in the same place and

19

then another. The man fell forward on his face, and turning, Jim heard the hoarse rattle of the automatic rifle.

Suddenly, Arnold's puckered scar twisted and his eyes widened.

"Jim!" he yelled. "The sub!"

Mayo sprang to the door. The sub had come up on the port bow, and the officer in the conning tower was staring at the ship in amazement. And it was no wonder. The *Natuna* was swinging idly on a flat sea, her deck a rattle of gunfire.

Arnold was yelling something about a sack, and Ponga Jim ran out on the bridge. Behind the corner of the wheelhouse was a canvas sack, and, jerking it open, he saw it was full of hand grenades. The sub was closing in for a better view, and a gun crew had swung the gun around to cover the ship. They were launching a boat, and a dozen men were climbing into it.

Ponga Jim jerked the pin and hurled the grenade. It hit the side of the submarine near the gun crew, and there was a terrific blast. But he had already thrown another. It fell short, but even as the gun crashed, he hurled another.

Their shot put a hole through the stack, but it was the only one they got a chance to fire. Arnold had rushed into the wing of the bridge and poured a stream of hot lead down at the conning tower and then clipped a couple of shots at the boat. Ponga Jim Mayo's next grenade lifted the boat out of the water, a blasted bunch of wreckage and struggling men.

The sub started to back off, obviously injured, but Jim hurled another grenade. The officer on the conning tower, apparently uninjured by Arnold's burst of rifle fire, had started down the ladder. In one horror-stricken moment his face showed white. Then there was a terrific concussion! The last grenade had fallen down the conning tower hatch.

William lowered his gun. His face was bleeding from a cut on his head.

"The marines have landed and have the situation well in hand!" he said.

20

"It wasn't a limey said that!" Mayo grunted. "That was an American."

"Righto!" William Arnold agreed.

Borg was getting to his feet. Mayo walked in and slugged him with the barrel of his automatic, which he'd retrieved and loaded.

"I'll tie this bird. He's wanted somewhere. Or we can kick him ashore in Sydney."

"Sydney?" Arnold said. "Why Sydney? This ship—"

"Listen, pal," Ponga Jim said patiently. "You're the British Intelligence or something, aren't you? Well, you want this activity stopped down here. You've prevented the landing of a lot of guns, and you've sunk an enemy submarine. Now I am informed that a certain gent high in official military circles at Sydney can buy arms and ammunition. For me, this represents profit, no loss. Now, unless you want to stage the War of 1812 all over again, we go to Sydney!"

Major William Arnold grinned. "This is no time to sever diplomatic relations with Ponga Jim Mayo," he said cheerfully. "Let me get some pants while you muster the rest of this crew, and we're off!"

He started down the ladder.

"Hey!" Jim said. "You know any dames in Sydney?"

"Just two," Arnold said. "Why?"

"Just two," Mayo said regretfully. "That's going to be tough. I'd hoped there would be enough for you, too!"

"Nuts!" Arnold said grimly, and walked down the ladder with his green pants flapping.

AUTHOR'S NOTE

AMURANG

On the bank of the river called Rano Rapo, is Amurang, a neat little town of some two thousand people, with white frame houses and a covered bridge crossing the river to Rumoon. Steamers of the K.P.M. line (the Koninklijki Paketvaart Maatschappij) call every four weeks en route from Surabaya. Another steamer from Makassar arrives every month. The hills around are thickly wooded except where cultivated. Coffee was the principal crop. There was a good road to the town of Menado, and one also to the town of Tondano. The mouth of the gulf on which Amurang is situated is roughly eight miles wide and penetrates about that distance inland. It is subject to violent squalls which can gather very suddenly over the mountains. These are called barats. Seamen often have other, less respectful names for them.

Such a sudden storm could be a very harrowing experience for a young man temporarily in command while the master and the chief mate were ashore on business. Fortunately there are no better seamen than the Bugis, and there were four of them on board on the *Semiramis* with Ponga Jim in this story.

ON THE ROAD TO
AMURANG

When he reached the road, Ponga Jim Mayo hesitated. Behind him, the wide, cool veranda of the Dutch Club echoed with soft laughter, the click of billiards, and the tinkle of glasses. There was a glow in the sky over Glandestan Way. But Ponga Jim's eyes turned toward the Punchar Wharves, where the *Semiramis* was tied.

His frown deepened. Balikpapan was no place for an empty ship. But it was better than having it at the bottom of the Molucca Passage, like the *Silver Lady*.

He hitched his shoulder to shift the heavy Colt automatic. Abruptly he faded into the shadows of the shrubbery, gun in hand.

"Jim," a voice called softly. "Hold it."

A drunken seaman was staggering down the road in stained dungarees and a grizzle of gray beard. He lurched closer, peering into Jim's face. Ponga Jim slipped the gun back into its holster.

"Damn you, William! If this is the way the British Intelligence works, the enemy will have to fumigate to get rid of you!"

Major Albert chuckled. Then he grew serious.

"Jim, don't you own the *Semiramis* now?"

"If you call a down payment owning it. But the way things

25

look, I'll never get a cargo for her. She's lying over at Punchar Wharves, as empty as my pockets will be tomorrow."

"What's the matter? Are the shippers afraid?"

Jim spat disgustedly. "Do you blame them? The *Arafura*, gone without a trace somewhere in the Sea of Celebes. The *Viti Queen*, last sighted off Flores. And now it's the *Silver Lady*, with a thousand tons of tin. In case you don't know, tin is valuable stuff. And a half dozen sailing craft gone."

"I know, Jim. Japan has threatened for years to take all the Far Eastern Dutch and British colonies if England went to war in Europe. There won't be a British or Dutch ship in the Indies within thirty days!"

Ponga Jim whistled. "Submarines?"

"We don't know. Subs demand a base."

Jim stared thoughtfully down the dark road. Thousands of islands, with lagoons, streams, and bays—

"You know all these damn islands, Jim. Now, if you were going to hide a submarine base, where would you do it?"

"There's a lot of places on Halmahera, on Buru, or Ceram. But there are places along the coast of Celebes, too. Nobody really knows these islands yet, William. But if I were going to base subs, I'd pick a spot on the Gulf of Tolo."

"That's Celebes, isn't it?" Major Albert asked.

"Yeah, an' not a track or clearing for miles and miles. A lonely country with cliffs and canyons six hundred feet straight up and down. Waterfalls and rapids that plunge over a wilderness of rocks. William, there's jungle back there that would turn a monkey's stomach sick with fear!"

"Listen, Jim," Major Albert said slowly. "I'm going to do you a favor. In return you can do me one. Li Wan Chuang has a consignment to deliver that means a contract for him. The *Silver Lady* was to handle it. The cargo goes to Amurang, Menado, and Wahai."

"What a pal you are! Between Menado and Wahai is the Molucca Passage. And at the bottom of the passage is the *Silver Lady*! You wouldn't put a guy on the spot, would you?"

The major grinned cheerfully. "You wanted a cargo, didn't you? All I ask is that you keep an eye open for a sub base."

"An' go prowling around the Gulf of Tolo and get my rudder shot off? Listen, you scenery bum. I'll keep my eyes open, but I'm not getting the *Semiramis* sunk running errands for you."

"Ssh!" Major Albert whispered suddenly. His voice became querulous, whining. "I sye, Guv'nor. Let a chap 'ave the price of a beer?"

"A beer?" Jim snapped harshly. "Here's a guilder. That ought to get you off the streets."

Jim spun on his heel and strode down the road. A car swung around a bend behind him. For an instant, its headlights sharply revealed three men. Ponga Jim's breath came sharply, and his hands slid from his pockets. He walked toward them.

Everyone in the islands knew Pete Lucieno. Short, fat, and oily, he participated in everything crooked in the Indies. With him were Sag Dormie and a huge man with a great moonlike face. Sag Dormie was known all too well in the islands. He had done time in the States and Australia. Some said he'd escaped from Devil's Island penal colony. He was kill-crazy. The big man was new. Looking up into his face, Ponga Jim felt his hackles rising. The man's eyes were dead.

Years before, in the States, Ponga Jim had been climbing a mountain. Pulling his head over the edge of a great, flat rock, he had found himself staring into the ugly eyes of a rattlesnake. That snake's eyes had been blank like these.

Ponga Jim looked at Pete and grinned insolently.

"What are you doing in Borneo? I thought they were putting a bounty on rats."

Pete Lucieno's eyes narrowed. "At least my ships have cargoes," he said softly. "They don't lie rusting at the dock."

"Yeah? Some people will carry anything for money. But you can have that stuff. I've got my own cargo. Sailing tomorrow for Amurang, Menado, and Wahai."

"*Where?*" Sag Dormie leaned forward intently. Jim noticed that Pete's eyes were eager. "Taking the Molucca Passage?"

"You bet! Want to come along? There's always room for rats in the bilges." Even as Jim watched Sag, he sensed the real danger was in the placid, fleshy man beside him.

Sag's hatchet face twisted into a sardonic smile.

"Through the Molucca Passage? I want to live a few years yet!"

"You are too sure of yourself, Captain," Lucieno said, his beady eyes gleaming from under his brows. "What of the *Silver Lady?*"

"Cap Marlin was my friend," Ponga Jim said coldly. "He was sunk. I only hope the guys who got him come after me."

He brushed by them and strode along the road. There was work to do and a cargo to load before daybreak. Yet he was uneasy. It had been only a matter of weeks since he had thrown Pete Lucieno for a loss by preventing the landing of munitions on the coast of New Guinea. Lucieno would never forgive that. What was more natural than that he should know of this threat that hung over the masts of British and Dutch shipping? Who else would dare locate a submarine base in the islands?

Jim walked up the gangway. A slim, dapper young Chinese stepped from the shadows behind the companionway.

"Captain Mayo? I am Li Wan Chuang. I have been informed you would transport some cargo for me. I took the responsibility of ordering it on the docks in readiness."

"Yeah—okay," Jim said, startled. "You surprised me. Chinese in these waters don't often speak good English. On second thought, neither do the white men."

"I went to the University of California for two years and took it very seriously. Then I went to the University of Southern California for two years. Now I take nothing seriously."

"We're going to get along," Ponga Jim grinned. "Do you know the chance we're taking?"

Li nodded. "But I must make delivery at once. And you have a reputation for getting results, Captain Mayo."

"It'll take more than that," Jim said crisply. He spun on his heel. "Mr. Millan! Get those hatches open and tell Haynes to power the winches."

It was hours later when he went below. The *Semiramis* was already dipping her bow into the heavy seas. The deck was still a confusion of lines and gear. It was going to be good to lie down. And he'd need all the rest he could get.

Opening the door, he stepped into his cabin. The wind caught the door, jerking it from his hand. He turned and pushed it shut.

When he looked around again, he stared into a gun muzzle. Beyond Sag Dormie, Pete Lucieno and the other man were sitting on a couch.

Jim hesitated. It was only for the flicker of an eye, but he found there wasn't a chance to shoot it out. Sag had him covered, yet was out of the line of fire of Lucieno and the big man. Ponga Jim relaxed.

"Visitors, I see. Just where do you boys think you're going?"

"Dussel thought this would be a good way to go to—to Menado," Sag said. "So we moved in when you weren't looking. I've been wanting to see how tough you were." He struck suddenly, smashing the back of his hand across Jim's lips.

Ponga Jim felt something burst inside and then dribble away, leaving him cold with anger. But Sag Dormie's gun was steady, and he did not move. Lucieno had a gun out, too. Mayo tasted blood in his mouth. He started to lift his hand to his mouth. The gun butt was just inside his coat—

"He's got a gun, Sag," Lucieno said. "In a shoulder holster. He carries it so always."

Sag jerked the gun from Mayo's holster and stuck it in his belt.

"I'll handle this. You won't need a gun anymore, Captain Ponga Jim Mayo."

Dussel moved his big body, and the settee creaked.

"You are to proceed as if nothing has happened, Captain

Mayo," he said. "You will go to Amurang, discharge cargo there, and then go on to Menado. I trust you will be discreet. Otherwise it might be necessary to take steps."

"You think you'll get away with this?" Jim queried casually. "You got to go topside sometime. What happens when the crew finds out?"

Dussel smiled, his pulpy flesh folding back like sodden dough.

"They know already. The last two cases you hoisted aboard contained my men. By now they have taken command. Your crew will do the work. My men will superintend it. Job Dussel does not make mistakes."

"I wonder about that. Do you think I'm going to take this lying down? And when this is over, what happens?"

"It is immaterial to me how you take this. When this is over, you and your ship will lie at the bottom of the Molucca Passage."

Dussel's voice was utterly final. For the first time in his life, Ponga Jim felt a rush of desperation. His eyes met Dussel's and fastened there. In the gross, white body before him was cold brutality, a ruthlessness almost reptilian. This man would stop at nothing.

Ponga Jim pushed the cap back on his head and slipped his thumbs behind the broad leather belt.

"Nothing to lose, eh?" he said. "I like it that way, Herr Dussel. You guys can pilot this ship. These are dangerous waters. But if I get knocked off anyway, what's it to me?"

Dussel's heavy-lidded eyes gleamed.

"I thought you would understand, Captain. You will obey orders carefully. You have heard of the Malay boot, Captain? It is child's play to some of the tortures I could use. If you don't obey—" He smiled. "But you will."

Ponga Jim shrugged. "You win."

Job Dussel's face remained folded back in a flabby smile.

Turning, Ponga Jim went topside. Daylight had come, and the sun was sparkling on the choppy sea. Thoughtfully, he climbed the companionway to the wheelhouse.

Slug Brophy, his chief mate, was standing watch. His tough, hard-bitten features were surly. In either wing of the bridge lounged a man with a Luger automatic. There was another in the wheelhouse. When Jim walked into the chart room, the man followed to the door, standing aside to let Brophy enter.

"Keep everything quiet, Slug," Jim said. "We hold this course until we get out of the strait. We're calling at Amurang and Menado before we make the Molucca Passage, then south to Wahai."

Ponga Jim paused. The guard was still standing in the door. Jim's finger touched the chart.

"I expect Herr Dussel to take over after we get into the passage." Jim touched the chart again, and his voice was precise. "We'll have to be careful right here. It's a bad spot, where things usually happen. Until then it should be plain sailing."

Slug nodded. "Okay, Cap. I get it."

The days were bright and sunny. The old *Semiramis* rolled along over the sea, doing her ten knots without a hitch. The crew moved carefully. Ponga Jim slept on the settee in the chart room. No further words were spoken. Yet he knew the crew was ready and waiting. But they didn't get a chance. Herr Dussel remained below, usually in conference with Lucieno.

Sag Dormie was wearing two guns openly now, and there were ten armed white men. Slowly Ponga Jim's spirits ebbed, but he continued to watch. There was bound to be a break.

It was almost midnight, and he was to go on watch. He swung his feet down from the settee. Pulling on his woven-leather sandals, he heard the lookout sound the bells, warning of a ship to starboard.

Instantly he was on his feet. He could see the squat, powerful mate on the bridge. Not far away, the two guards engaged in low-voiced conversation. The guard in the wheelhouse was nodding against the bulkhead. It was one chance in a million, and Jim took it.

His hand groped for the switch controlling the light on the topmast. He began switching the light on and off, his eyes intent on the topmasts of the approaching ship.

31

LI WAN CHUANG, BALIKPAPAN, ENEMY
ABOARD GET WORD M. W. A. SIGNED MAYO.

He was sending the message the second time when one of
the guards saw the flickering light. As the guard leaped from
the deck of the wheelhouse, Jim slammed a vicious right to his
chin. He toppled back. Just as the two guards jammed in the
port door, Jim sprang out. A bullet shrieked after him. He
went down the companionway and crashed into Herr Dussel,
just issuing from the captain's cabin.

Mayo hurled a terrific right at Dussel, and missed. A smashing right sprawled him to the deck. He sprang to his feet,
amazed at the huge man's astonishing speed. Jim stabbed out
with a wicked left. He might as well have hit a wall. A powerful
blow struck him on the chin, and he rolled back against the
bulkhead. Before he could get in the clear, two more vicious
punches hit him.

Staggering, Jim tried to crouch. An uppercut jerked him
erect. A lightninglike right cross sent him spinning. Dussel
followed, for a killing punch. Jim struggled to his feet, rolled
away, and then circled warily.

He wanted to tear into the giant, battle him to the wall, and
beat him down. But there was no time for that. Even if he
won, there were the other men.

Job Dussel was crowding him into a corner. Jim backed away
carefully. Suddenly he reached back and grabbed the rail. He
kicked out viciously. The blow caught Dussel in the chest,
staggering him across the deck.

With the agility of a panther, Jim leaped over the rail to the
main deck.

He landed running. A bullet smashed into the hatch coaming
nearby. Another one whipped by his ears. He threw himself to
the deck, landing on one shoulder. He rolled over to momentary safety behind a winch.

Something hard lay under his hand—a wooden wedge used

for battening a hatch. The sky had clouded over, and a few spattering drops of rain were falling. In the glare of occasional lightning, he could see four men with rifles on the bridge. Two more were on the captain's deck, where he had battled Dussel.

Coming forward were Sag Dormie and three thugs. Behind him was the tightly battened number one hatch. Beyond that was the forecastle, and above it the forecastle head, and nothing else but a spare ventilator lashed to the steam-pipe housing and a small hatch into the forepeak. Of course there was the anchor winch. But he couldn't see a possible hiding place.

Instinctively Jim knew these men were out to kill him. Crawling to his feet, grasping the wedge, he waited. At a distant flash of lightning, he hurled the wedge. He had the satisfaction of hearing the solid smack of wood against flesh. A gun roared, but it was a chance shot. He knew he hadn't been seen.

He reached the forepeak and waited tensely. Aft, on the bridge, he heard Dussel roaring.

"Go ahead, you fools! He's not armed!"

It was only a matter of minutes. He was trapped. The forepeak was a hole without exit. Behind him was the bow, dipping slightly with the roll of the ship.

He heard a moan on the ladder to port and then one to starboard. He crouched. A thought struck him. He crept close to the rail. He heard two men reach the forecastle head on the port side, not twenty feet away. Someone else was just stepping from the companionway, even closer.

Ponga Jim knew he could hesitate no longer. He crawled through the rail and lowered himself over the side of the ship. The bow dipped. For an instant he felt a wave of panic.

Clinging desperately, he grabbed through the hole of the bow chock. A slip meant a plunge into the dark waters below. He shifted his other hand to the chock and then lowered himself onto the flukes of the anchor.

It was a wild gamble, but his only chance. He thanked all the fates that the *Semiramis* was blunt-bowed. A light flashed on, off, and then on again.

33

"Chief!" Dormie shouted, his voice incredulous. "He's gone. He's disappeared!"

"Search the forepeak, you damned numbskull!" Dussel roared. "If that devil gets away, I'll kill you. Search the forecastle, too."

Crouching on the flukes of the anchor, Ponga Jim waited tensely. The old barge would soon be dipping her bows under. After that his time would be short. Feet pounded on the deck. He heard the men cursing.

"Maybe he slipped past," Dormie grumbled. "It's dark enough. He couldn't hide here."

A wave splashed over Ponga Jim's feet. The bow dipped and black water swept over him. He clung to the anchor, shivering.

Minutes passed. Feet mounted the ladder again. He heard a man muttering. Then the fellow walked across the deck and stood by the bulwark overhead.

Another sea drenched Jim to the skin. He clung to the flukes, trying to keep his teeth still. The ship gave a sickening lunge. His feet fell clear, and for a moment he hung clear as the bow lifted. Then lightning flashed.

As he pulled himself up, he saw a man leaning over the bulwark. It was Longboy, one of his own crew.

With a roar, a huge sea swept over Jim. The *Semiramis* lifted her bow.

"Psst!" he hissed sharply. Longboy looked down, startled. "Get a line," Jim whispered. "It's the skipper." The man wheeled around from the rail. In an instant, a line dangled in front of Jim's face. He went up, hand over hand. Just as the bow dipped under another big one, Jim tumbled on deck.

"Lookout!" a hoarse voice shouted. "Come to the bridge."

"Getting too rough here," Jim commented. "They'll have you stand watch there. Tell Brophy I'm safe, but be careful. Then you three stand by. I'm going to start something, and damned quick!"

As Longboy hurried aft, Ponga Jim went down the companionway, into the forecastle. What he wanted now was a weapon. It was dark inside.

Suddenly a cigarette glowed. It was a guard. In the faint glow of the cigarette he saw the glint of metal. The guard's head turned.

Ponga Jim swung. He had only the mark of the glowing cigarette, but it was enough. He felt bone crunch under his fist. The man crumpled. Jim struck a match.

A frightened face peered from the curtains of a bunk, then another.

"Out of those bunks now!" Jim snapped. "I'm taking over." He picked up the guard's Luger and fished two clips from his pocket. He turned on the powerful lascar behind him. "Where are these fellows? You just came off watch, didn't you?"

Abdul nodded. "Two mans in crew's mess. Two mans below. One man on poop deck. Three on bridge. Small fat man, he sleep. Two other mans sleep. Big fat man, he talk this Dormie."

"Right, Abdul, you get that man on the poop deck. Then you, Hassan, Mohamet, Chino, get the two men below. Chino, slip on this man's coat and cap. Go to the ladder an' call them. They'll come up."

"Yes, Tuan. We understand." The four men slipped out on deck, their naked feet soundless in the rising storm.

Ponga Jim turned to the two men who remained. They were short and powerful men, alike as two peas. Both wore green turbans.

"Sakim, you and Selim go aft. One of you tell Millan. Then meet me by the crew's mess."

Dampness touched his face. He stood grasping the rail. A wave, black and glistening, rolled up and then swirled by. A storm of spray swept across the deck. He tasted salt on his lips. Rain and spray beat against his face. The green starboard light stared down at him, a solitary eye. It was going to be a bad time before morning.

*   *   *

He started aft, walking fast, his knees bending to the roll of the ship. Job Dussel wanted a showdown, and he was going to get it. Jim couldn't wait for Menado, not even for Amurang. Maybe his message would get to Li Wan Chuang, maybe not. It was a chance he couldn't afford to take. Major Albert had said that not a British or Dutch ship would arrive for days.

What the plan was, he could only guess. One thing he knew—they had done for Cap Marlin and the *Silver Lady*. Now they threatened peaceful vessels that carried no munitions, no soldiers, only traded quietly among the islands. Ponga Jim's jaw set hard, and his eyes narrowed.

Suddenly he laughed. He caught the rail of the companionway to the deck outside his cabin and swung up. His hand was on the door, the Luger ready. A light flashed across him from the bridge. The Luger snapped up and roared. The light crashed out. He heard the tinkle of falling glass and then someone moaned. There was a shout from the wheelhouse.

Ponga Jim jerked the door open.

"Get 'em up!" he roared. He stopped, amazed. The room was empty!

He sprang inside and rushed to the adjoining cabin. It was also empty. Wheeling, he raced for the door. From above came a shout, a shot. Aft, he heard sounds of confusion. He leaped to the deck outside his cabin door. A blast of wind and spray struck his face.

A guard stood in the opening of the amidships passage. Even as Jim's eyes caught the flash of movement, the rifle roared. A shot clipped by his head. Jim fired. The man staggered and then jerked up the rifle again. Jim fired again. The man dropped the rifle and grabbed his stomach with both hands.

Jim made the bridge in two jumps. He came face to face with Brophy. The Irishman was grinning.

"Everything under control, Cap! You got one, I got one, an' the other got away. Get Dussel, Dormie?"

Jim's brow creased. He was staring aft. Something had slipped up somewhere.

"No. They weren't in the cabin."

36

He strode into the wheelhouse. Longboy was standing there with a rifle. The man at the wheel was grinning.

"Steady as she goes," Jim said. He turned to Longboy. "Get in the chart room and open the port aft. Watch carefully. Shoot to kill."

Abdul appeared around the corner of the deckhouse. Behind him were Chino and Hassan. When they reached the bridge, Ponga Jim looked quickly from one to the other.

"Two we kill. Mohamet, he die, too."

Ponga Jim sighed wearily. "Chino, you stand by here. Brophy, keep this bridge. Don't let anybody but our men come up."

Jim slipped cartridges into the Luger. He started down the companionway. It was blowing a gale now. Every few minutes the sea came roaring over the bow and swept aft, gurgling in the scuppers.

Selim was standing in the door of the galley when they went aft. Sakim was just beyond. Both were watching the door of the crew's mess.

"How many?" Ponga Jim asked.

"Two. They stay still, Tuan. Something funny."

Ponga Jim stepped quickly to the mess room door. The two men sitting at the table were dead. One was the man he had shot in the passage. The other was probably one of those killed below. They had been propped up to delay pursuit.

Five men killed, and one of his own. Gunner Millan came running down the passage, gun in hand.

"Where'd they go? What the devil's happening?"

Ponga Jim shrugged grimly. "I wish I knew. We got five of them. There are five left, besides Dussel, Lucieno, and Sag Dormie. We got them outnumbered two to one, but half our boys are on duty."

"Listen, Cap," said Slug Brophy, running. "That guy Dussel radioed some ship. I heard him tell Lucieno they were going to meet us in Himana Bay."

"That's the answer," Jim cried. "Dussel decided to hole up until help comes. He doesn't want to waste his men."

"But where is he?" Millan asked.

"Somewhere aft. Either the poop or below." Ponga Jim turned to Brophy. "You better get back on that bridge. No traffic in here, but you never can tell. Swing north about thirty degrees. I'll give those guys at Himana something to think about."

Brophy went forward, teetering with the roll of the ship. Jim motioned to Selim.

"You and Sakim stand by with the rifles. If one of them shows his noggin, blast it off. Abdul, you and Hassan turn in and get some sleep. Gunner, radio Amurang, Gorontalo, or someplace. Get in touch with Major Albert or Li Wan Chuang. Try to get some dope on a converted merchantman."

"You don't think it's a sub?" Millan asked.

"If it was, they'd never pick Himana Bay. There's a native village, and a sub would attract too much attention. It's only a few hours across the peninsula to Gorontalo. An armed freighter could lay there a week."

Dawn broke, with the sun bright and the sea choppy. Ponga Jim was drinking coffee in the wheelhouse when Selim came up with a rush.

"Men gone!" he shouted. "He take boat off poop. All gone!"

"What?" Jim demanded. "Well, maybe it's good riddance."

He stood up and raised the binoculars.

"Selim! Get below and turn out the crew. Send Millan to me."

Gunner Millan came running. He was minus a shirt, but had strapped on a gun. Ponga Jim turned quickly.

"Go aft and jerk the cover off number five. Then hoist out that gun you'll find in the 'tween decks under canvas. I want it mounted aft. You know how to handle that. Lucky this damned old barge is a war veteran and still carries her gun mounting."

"Where'd you get the gun?" Millan asked.

Jim grinned. "I knocked over a load of munitions a few weeks ago. That gun looked good, so I kept it and sold the rest.

Unless I'm mistaken, we're going to have the fight of our lives. I didn't get the idea until Selim told me Dussel and his boys got away—"

"Got away?" Millan cried.

"Yeah, they launched that lifeboat from the after wheelhouse. It was a gamble, but they took it. The weather broke about four bells. They'll contact that cruiser of theirs."

"It'll take them a couple of days to get to Himana," Millan exclaimed. "By that time we'll be in Amurang."

"No," Jim said. "There's a radio in that boat. Himana Bay isn't more than thirty or forty minutes from where they left us. Even if the radio wouldn't do it, they could sail with the breeze they've had since they started." He pointed with the hand that held the glasses. "There's smoke on the horizon. Unless I miss my guess, that will be them."

Millan clambered down, and Ponga Jim crossed to the wheel.

"Swing back to eighty degrees. At four bells, change her again to one hundred and thirty degrees."

Longboy mumbled the course back to him, and Jim walked back to the bridge. It was going to be a tight race. Changing course was going to bring them up on him faster. But it was going to take him in close to the coast, nearer Amurang, in waters he knew and where his shallower draft would be an advantage. The other ship was doing at least fifteen knots to the *Semiramis*'s ten.

Slug Brophy came up, looking tough.

"This is going to be good, Cap. Ever see Millan handle one of those big guns?"

"He used to be on the *Hood*. I never saw him work."

"That guy could knock the buttons off your shirt with a sixteen-inch gun." Brophy chuckled. "He could knock off anything with our four-inch gun."

Ponga Jim glanced aft. "She's coming up fast. Looks like about forty-eight hundred tons."

39

"Yeah," Brophy muttered. "And riding fairly low. But she's not loaded by a damn sight."

Ponga Jim pointed to a spot on the chart.

"See that? That point is Tanjung Bangka. Right about here is a patch of reef. She lies in about a fathom and a half. Loaded the way we are, she will give us just enough clearance. You're taking her over."

"Maybe she's not so deep now, Cap. What if there ain't that much water?"

"Then it's going to be tough. We're going over, and I only hope that monkey back there follows us!"

Ponga Jim ran down and hurried aft. Selim, Sakim, Abdul, and Hassan were all standing by with rifles. Millan crouched at the gun with two men.

Smoke leaped from the bow of the other vessel. A shot whistled overhead. Another blasted off to starboard.

"Get that gun if you can," Jim said quietly. He picked up a rifle. "I want that monkey in the crow's nest."

Whipping the rifle to his shoulder, he fired three times. The man in the crow's nest slumped forward. His rifle slid from his hands.

Millan's gun roared. Jim saw the shell smash into the bulkhead of the forward deckhouse. The gun crashed again. At the same instant a shell blasted open number four hatch, ripping a winch and ventilator to bits.

"There goes my profit on this trip," Jim said. "I never did care for war."

Millan's gun crashed. They saw the shell shatter the enemy's gun. Millan fired again. A shot struck the *Semiramis* amidships. Mayo winced.

He ran to the rail and glanced at the faint discoloration of the reef.

"A fathom and a half is right," he said cheerfully. "I must report that to the Hydrographic Office. Get that after gun when she strikes the reef. When we swing alongside, let them board us. They will, because they'll be sinking!"

"Are you nuts?" Millan protested.

*   *   *

There was a terrific crash astern, a grinding scream as the bow of the pursuing ship lifted over the reef. With a tortured rending of steel plates, the big freighter slid over the reef, canted sharply to starboard. Ponga Jim turned and raced for the bridge.

"Hard to port!" he yelled at Brophy. "Swing around and come in alongside."

Millan's gun banged, then again. Someone was shouting from the bridge. Rifle shots swept the deck of the *Semiramis*. Back aft, Millan was coolly battering the larger ship to pieces. The shells were smashing the superstructure into a mountain of twisted steel.

The *Semiramis* slid alongside. Ponga Jim dived for the ladder, gun in hand. A bullet slammed by his head and went whining off over the sea. He snapped an effective shot at a big German sailor.

The main deck was a pitched battle. Abandoning his gun, Millan was leading the lascars to stem the tide of men leaping from the rail of the wrecked ship. From the bridge, Slug Brophy was working two guns, firing from the hips.

Ponga Jim fired twice. Something struck him a terrific blow on the head. He pulled himself erect, feeling the warm rush of blood down his face. Something smashed into the bulkhead beside him and he found himself staring at a mushroomed bullet. With an effort, he pulled himself around.

Sag Dormie was standing on the edge of the ruined number four hatch. Just as Jim looked up, Sag's gun blossomed fire. Miraculously, he missed. Ponga Jim's gun swung up, roaring a stream of fire and lead.

Blank astonishment swept over Sag's face. Still trying to lift his gun, he toppled back into the black maw of the hatch.

Shooting and slugging furiously, Ponga Jim leaped into the brawl on the main deck. Hassan was down, his body riddled. Big Abdul stabbed and ripped a heavy knife at a circle of enemies. Jim's shot cut one of them down. Another man wheeled to face him. Mayo slammed him with the barrel of the gun. The man wilted.

But where the hell was Dussel? Blood streaming down his face, Jim stared around. He saw him, standing on the bridge of the other ship. As he looked up, Job Dussel saw him and beckoned.

Jim cleared both rails at a leap. Job met him at the top, his white, pulpy face wrinkled in a smile. Then the big man leaped.

But this time Jim was ready. Rolling under a left, he slammed each fist into the big man's body. Dussel crowded him back, swinging. When he tried to duck he was caught with a wicked uppercut that knocked him back against the wheelhouse. There was no chance for boxing. It was a matter of standing toe to toe on the narrow bridge and slugging.

Dussel hooked a vicious right that knocked him to his knees and then shot out a kick that Jim barely evaded. Staggering to his feet, Ponga Jim was blinded by the blood from his scalp wound. He scarcely felt the terrific driving force of those blows that rained about his head and body. Driving in, he weaved and bobbed. He felt only the killing desire to batter that gross body against the bulkhead, to drive him back, back, back!

Knocked sprawling to hands and knees, Dussel toppled forward, and Jim sprang up behind him. The big man was on his feet in an instant. But Jim whipped a short, wicked right hook into that rising pulpy face.

Like a brick landing in a pool, the big man's features seemed to splash. With a cry of mortal agony, Dussel sprang back, blood streaming from a fearful gash across his cheek.

Ponga Jim stared. The huge, hard body, seemingly so soft, was impregnable, almost beyond injury. But the face—

Jim crowded closer, swinging both hands. A blow staggered him. But he went under and whipped up a left hook that bared Dussel's cheekbone. A terrific right knocked Dussel sprawling along the bridge.

Someone was shouting at Jim. He looked up, dazed. A slim white cutter had swept up, scarcely a half dozen yards away. Standing on the bow was Major Albert, immaculate in a white and gold uniform!

"Jump, you slug-minded clown!" Major Albert yelled. "That damned old scow is sinking under your feet! Stop playing slap hands with that beef trust slugger!"

"William," Jim gulped. He suddenly felt relaxed and empty inside. "You look sweet enough to kiss. Am I seeing stars or are those gold buttons?"

"Jump, damn you!" Albert roared. "If you don't, I'll come after you!"

Jim stared around. The water was creeping over the decking of the bridge!

Jim sprang to the rail of the bridge and off into the water. Panting and dripping, he was hauled aboard the cutter. He could see the sturdy old *Semiramis* standing off. The crew let out a cheer and dived into the water, swimming for the cutter.

"Look!" Major Albert said suddenly.

On the bridge of the sinking freighter, Job Dussel had tottered to his feet. His wide, repulsive face was horribly smashed and bloody. The white shirt hanging around him in shreds revealed his great body. Instead of fat, enormous bulges of muscle hung over his arms and shoulders. His torso was like the trunk of a vast tree!

Staggering to the rail, Dussel toppled blindly into the water. With a grinding crash, as though it had waited for that instant, the freighter slipped down into deeper water. Only swirls of water marked the spot. . . .

Ponga Jim turned to Major Albert.

"William," he said. "I got so busy there at last, I never did find out where your sub base was located."

"You said the Gulf of Tolo before you started," William grinned. "That gave me a lead. Then the *Valapa Bay* relayed the message you sent with the mast light. I knew if they were

43

aboard the *Semiramis,* it was because they had to get to the Molucca Passage, or to some boat en route. That pointed in the same direction. We investigated and found the submarine base.

"You see, Dussel and Lucieno didn't dare show themselves on a British ship. The Dutch were watching for them, too. Then the boys found you were going to Amurang, Menado, and Wahai, so they slipped aboard. Job Dussel sank the *Silver Lady.* He also sank those other ships, sank them without a chance. He was aiming at paralyzing the entire trade of the islands—and he came damned near success. He was a brute, all right!"

Ponga Jim Mayo wiped the back of his hand across his bloody mouth.

"Yeah, he was a brute," he said. "But, William"—Jim pointed back at the reef, where the waters were stirring slightly over the rocks—"that guy could fight! Boy, how that guy could fight!"

AUTHOR'S NOTE

BANGGAI

The Banggai group of islands were inhabited at the time of which I write by a very primitive people living in the mountains and avoiding contact with the Muslims along the shores.

These islands were one of the best sources of ebony, a dark, beautiful wood much used for carving and furniture. The islands are also a source of mica. Gum and rattan are brought from the forests. Maize, tobacco, sugar cane, and sago are cultivated. Many of the islands are high and thickly wooded.

The Banggai Islands and the Sula group lie eastward of Celebes, and at the time of which I write the area was imperfectly surveyed, so navigation was conducted with caution.

FROM HERE TO
BANGGAI

"**Y**ou know, William," Ponga Jim Mayo said drily, "I'm getting so I hate to see that handsome pan of yours showing itself around. Every time you come around me I end up getting shot at."

Major Arnold smiled blandly. "Never give it a thought, Jim. I don't. They can't shoot a man that was born to be hung."

"Huh!" Ponga Jim emptied his glass and reached for the bottle. "That's a swell crack from the guy whose bacon I've saved at least twice. If it wasn't for me you'd have lost the war right here in the East Indies. And you, a British intelligence officer, razzing me. It pains me, William, it really pains me!"

"All of which," Major Arnold continued, ignoring him, "reminds me. How did you ever get that 'Ponga' tied to your name?"

Mayo grinned complacently and settled back in his chair. "It's a long story, William. A story that will make your pink British ears pinker, and much too rough for your sensitive moral condition. However, over in Africa, there's a place called Gabon, and in Gabon is a town called Ponga-Ponga. Now, a few years past over in Ponga-Ponga was a young man named Mayo, and—"

"Jim," Major Arnold whispered suddenly. "Who are those men at the next table?"

Ponga Jim chuckled. "I was wondering how long it would take the British Intelligence to wake up to those lugs," he said.

Then he said guardedly, "Believe me, those guys are a barrel-ful of hell for you and me. Despite the obvious military bearing of at least two of them, those gents are merely innocent passengers on the good ship *Carlsberg*. You may remember the *Carlsberg* is from Copenhagen, but not so many days past her home port was Bremerhaven.

"The chap with the bulge behind his belt is a commercial traveler, even though he looks like a member of the Nazi Gestapo. The lean, hard-faced guy isn't a naval officer, but only a man traveling for his health. The—"

"Ssh!" Major Arnold whispered. "The fat one is coming over."

The man's face was rotund, and his round belly was barely controlled by a heavy leather belt. He looked jolly and lazy until you saw his eyes. They were small, and hard as bits of steel. Like the others, he wore whites and a sun helmet.

He stopped beside their table. "I beg your pardon," he said, smiling slowly, "but I accidentally heard your friend call you Ponga Jim. Aren't you master of the *Semiramis*?"

"Yeah," Jim acknowledged. "Have a seat."

The German seated himself between them, smiling contentedly. "And your friend?"

Major Arnold waved a deprecatory hand, looking very much the neat, well-bred Englishman. "My name is Girard, William Girard," he said. "I'm trying my hand at pearl buying."

"And mine is Romberg," the fat man said. Then he turned to Jim. "Isn't it true, Captain, that you clear for Bonthain and Menado soon? Captain van Raalt, the pilot, told me your cargo was for those ports. My friends and I are interested, as we have some drilling machinery for shipment to Banggai."

"Banggai's on my route," Jim said. "You and your friends want to go along as passengers?"

Romberg nodded. "I can start the cargo moving right away, if you wish," he said.

"The quicker the better," Mayo said, getting up. "We're moving off as soon as that cargo's stowed."

Romberg, after shaking hands with both of them, rejoined his friends.

"Well, William," Jim said softly, when they had reached the street, "what do you make of it?"

"That cargo to Banggai looks like a load of trouble, if you ask me," the major said grimly. "Cancel it. I didn't know they were here yet, but I knew the Gestapo was out to get you. They know you messed up that New Guinea deal and their plans here."

Ponga Jim shrugged. "So what? Cargo doesn't lay around waiting for a guy. I'll take my chances and—" he smiled grimly, his eyes hard, "they'll take theirs!"

"Don't say you weren't warned," Arnold said resignedly. "Those Gestapo men are cruel, relentless, vindictive. You wrecked their plans, and now you're marked for death."

"William," Ponga Jim said pointedly, "I need that money. Everything I got in the world is in that old tub down there by the dock. I got to win or go down swinging—and I'm winning!"

He turned and walked rapidly down the street. Over six feet tall, Ponga Jim weighed two hundred pounds and carried it like a featherweight. In the officer's cap, the faded khaki suit, and woven-leather sandals he looked tough, hard-bitten. His jaw was strong, and his face was tanned by wind, sun, and brine.

Arnold shrugged. "Maybe," he said softly, "maybe he can do it. If ever a man could go through hell barefooted, that's the one!"

Makassar was dozing in the heat of a tropical evening. Like many tropical towns it can sleep for weeks or months and then suddenly explode with volcanic force, releasing all its pent-up violence in one mad burst and then falling quietly into the doldrums once more.

Now it was quiet, but with an uneasy stillness like the hush before a storm. Ponga Jim stopped on the end of the Juliana Quay, and Slug Brophy walked up.

"Been around the joints?" Jim asked him.

49

Brophy nodded. He was a short, thickset man with enormously broad shoulders and a massive chest. His head was set on a short, thick neck. His heavy jaw was always black with beard. He was wearing whites, with shirt-sleeves rolled up and his cap at an angle.

"Yeah," Brophy said, "but I came back. I don't like the looks of things. Everything is quiet enough, but some of the bad ones are looking wise. I saw Gunong, Stello, and Hankins. They've all been drinking a little, and they've got something up their sleeves."

"Crew aboard?" Jim asked.

"All but Li Chuang, the Chinese steward you picked up in Perth. He's ashore picking up something extra special for you."

Jim nodded. "I'm going to look him up. We're getting under way as soon as this new cargo gets loaded. The Gunner watching it?"

Brophy nodded. "Cap," he asked, "is there anything funny about this cargo?"

"Trouble. Those Nazis want me out of the picture. This whole deal is a trap. But they pay in advance."

Brophy grinned widely. "In advance, huh? Okay, Cap. Let's go!"

Ponga Jim turned and started back up the street. A month before, he had bought the *Semiramis* in Melbourne, a battered old tramp with too many years behind her. From the beginning, there had been trouble finding a steward. Then he had stumbled across Li in Perth and had shipped the Chinese at once.

Since then life aboard ship had improved. Li knew how and where to buy supplies, and he always managed to save money. In short, he was too close to a miracle to have running around loose, Jim thought.

Jim was passing the Parakeet Nest, a dive near the waterfront, when he heard a fist smack and a rattle of Chinese in vigorous expostulation. His pulses jumped at the sound, and he wheeled, pushing through the swinging doors.

Hankins, a burly beachcomber with an evil reputation; Gunong, a Buginese; and Stello, a Portuguese Malay were gathered about, shouting. On the floor lay Li Chuang, his packages scattered about, his face livid with anger.

Hankins stood over him, kicking the slender Chinese in the ribs.

With one bound, Mayo was through the door. Gunong shouted and Hankins whirled, and even as he turned he unleashed a terrific right. It was a killing punch, and Jim Mayo was coming fast. It caught him full on the chin and sent him crashing against the wall. His head bounced, and he slid to the floor.

For just an instant, everyone stared, unbelieving. Then, with a roar, Burge Hankins leaped to finish the job. But that instant had been almost enough, and Jim rolled his head away from the wild kick launched by the raging beachcomber.

Hankins' recklessness cost him victory. The kick missed, and Mayo lurched drunkenly to his feet. The room swam before him in a smoky haze. A punch slid off the side of his head, and he staggered forward, fighting by instinct while Hankins wasted his fury in a mad rain of blows when one measured punch would have won.

Ponga Jim Mayo was out on his feet. The room circled him dizzily, and through the haze he saw the horror-stricken face of Li squatting on the floor, blood trickling through his lips.

Ponga Jim was punch drunk and he was still groggy, but suddenly he was a fighting man. With a growl like a wounded beast, he struck savagely. His left smashed into Hankins' face and knocked the surprised beachcomber against the bar with such driving force that his head bobbed, just in time to meet the sweeping right that lifted him off his feet and knocked him bloody and broken into a corner.

Then Ponga Jim whirled around. Half crouched, his eyes blazing with an unholy fire, he faced the crowded dive. Swaying drunkenly, he stared, hands working.

51

*   *   *

The startled crowd stared, and the giant Gunong ran a thin tongue over his parched lips. Feverishly, his eyes sought the door. Ponga Jim took a step forward, and then, with the speed of light, he leaped.

Gunong's knife slashed out. A half inch closer would have ripped Ponga Jim's stomach open. But it ripped his shirt from side to side and left a red slash across the skin. Then Jim was upon him with a hail of blows that swept down almost too fast for the eye to follow. In seconds Gunong was out cold.

But Ponga Jim was playing no favorites. He smashed out and knocked a Buginese cutthroat reeling. Someone leaped astride of his back and he grabbed the man by the head and threw him bodily over his shoulder into the wall. With a roar of fury Jim waded into the crowd. Blows rained about him. Men screamed with pain, and he felt hands grasping at his legs. He kicked back desperately, and somebody cried out.

With a leap, Jim reached the bar. He smashed a bottle over the head of the nearest man. Maddened faces, streaked with blood and sweat, massed around him. A fist struck his chin, staggering him. He came up with a broken chair leg.

The room was a riot of fighting and insane fury.

Suddenly Jim remembered the gun, and his hand jerked up and ripped open the holster. Then he cursed with fury. To hell with it! He slammed a fist into a face nearby, grabbed the man by the throat and jerked him to arm's length overhead, and heaved him out into the crowd. He was swaying dizzily, and suddenly he was conscious that his arms were heavy, that he was fighting with his back to the wall. Still they crowded around him.

The floor was littered with injured men, but still he didn't use the gun. For an instant, they drew back, staring at him with malevolence.

A big Dyak was down, his face a smear of blood. He tried to get up and then fell back. The pack sensed a kill. Like wolves about an injured bull, they circled warily. They were closing in now.

Ponga Jim Mayo crouched, waiting. He still had the gun, but like a true fighting man, he hated to use it. Guns were his business, but a fight was a fight, and gang fight or otherwise, Ponga Jim Mayo had always won. Desperate, bitter, bloody, but always he and his crew had come out on the top.

Stello, who had hung back, now came forward. He was clutching a kris, and his lips were parted in a sneer of hatred. Yet, even as Jim waited, knowing the next attack would be the last, he realized something was behind this, something more than a mere attack on his cook. These men were cutthroats, but they were organized cutthroats. They hadn't gathered here by accident. Even as he realized that, his mind leaped to his ship, to Romberg, to . . .

Stello smiled, his beady eyes gleaming maliciously. "You want beg now, Ponga Jim? You want die now?"

The big half-caste took a step forward. Behind him, the semicircle moved forward. In a split second they would attack!

Ponga Jim's hand, out of sight behind the bar, fell across the handle of the shot-filled hose that the bartender used in case of brawls. In that instant, Stello lunged. But as he lunged the loaded hose swept up and lashed him across the face!

Ponga Jim Mayo heard the bones crunch, saw the big man's nose flatten and his face turn blue with that vicious blow. And in that instant the doors burst open and Slug Brophy leaped in, followed by the crew of the *Semiramis*. What followed was a slaughter.

Somewhere outside a policeman stopped. He looked at the door. He saw a notorious cutthroat stagger outside, trying desperately to pull a knife from his chest. Then the officer turned and disappeared into the darkness. This was no place for an honest policeman.

The streets were silent and still very suddenly, as a silent body of men walked out on Juliana Dock and aboard the *Semiramis*.

The Gunner was standing by the gangway, gun in hand. Ponga Jim came up, staggering. His face was smeared with dried blood and his shirt was gone. The holster with the gun was still hanging from his shoulder. As the men trooped slowly aboard, Ponga Jim turned to the Gunner.

"All aboard, Millan? If they are, get the anchor up. There'll be hell from here to Batavia for this night's work." He glanced across at the *Carlsberg*, her shadow looming large in the darkness.

He walked to his cabin and fell across the bed. There were things to be done, but they would have to wait. With a sigh Ponga Jim fell asleep.

It was morning when he awoke. He took a shower, washing away the dried blood from his face and hair. Gingerly, he bathed a swollen lip and hand. There was a bad gash on his scalp, too, and a lump under one eye. Casually, he dressed then and checked his gun.

The morning sun struck him like a blow, and he stood still for a moment, looking out over the sea. It was calm, with the wind about force two. Ponga Jim climbed the ladder to the bridge. The Gunner came out of the wheelhouse. He looked worried, but brightened when he saw Mayo.

"Hi, Cap. Glad to see you around."

Jim grunted. "Yeah, I'm glad to be around."

"That must have been some fight!" Gunner exclaimed.

"That fight was a plant, a put-up job!" Ponga Jim looked off over the sea astern. To the south loomed the heavy shoulders of a mountainous island. "Kabalena?" he asked Gunner. "That's Batu Sengia, isn't it?"

"Yeah," Millan agreed. "We're doing okay. You want to take over now?"

Jim shook his head. "Hold it till noon. I'll take the twelve to four."

Ponga Jim walked into the wheelhouse and stood staring down at the chart spread on the table. Major Arnold had been right. That effort in the Parakeet Nest had been the first attempt. That failing, there would be something else. The only question was when and where. Soon his ship would be in Tioro Strait, then Wowoni Strait and the Banda Sea. These islands, Muna and Butung, were little known, their inhabitants strange tribes of Malay-speaking people who kept to themselves.

Ponga Jim had taken the cargo with the full knowledge that it meant trouble, confident of his ability to cope with it. Remembering the icy flecks in Romberg's eyes his scalp tightened. He glanced at the passenger list lying on the desk. Romberg, Kessler, and Braunig. Kessler was the thin, hard-faced man, Braunig the burly, silent fellow.

The Gunner came in. "How's it look, Jim?" he asked softly. "We got some tough babies aboard?"

"Yeah," Ponga Jim said. "Keep your eyes on them, and tell your watch to do the same thing. Keep a rod handy."

The Gunner slapped his waistband. "I got one." His brow wrinkled. "I'm more scared of that damned orangutan than I am of any of them."

"That *what*?" Jim wheeled. "Did you say orangutan?"

"Sure, didn't you know?" Millan was astonished. "Braunig says it's a pet. Biggest one I ever saw. He feeds it himself, won't let anybody else get close."

"Pet, is it?" Ponga Jim's left eyebrow squinted and his eyes narrowed. "In a strong cage?"

Millan nodded. "Yeah. It would be a hell of a thing to tackle in the dark. Or in the daytime, for that matter."

Mayo shrugged. "It won't get out. Put an extra lock on it. And if Braunig kicks, send him to me."

He watched the blunt-bowed *Semiramis* plow through the seas. Old she might be, but she was dependable. Ponga Jim knew that peace in the East Indies might erupt into war at any moment. The war that had thrown all Europe into arms and that threatened at any moment to turn cities into a smoking shambles, was already eating at the shores of these lonely

islands. Twice, Ponga Jim Mayo had been involved in attempts
to create strife here, at this furthest limit of the British Empire.

An American adventurer and master of tramp freighters,
Mayo preferred to mind his own business, settle his private
fights, and stay out of international affairs. But following the
sea in the Indies had never been a picnic, and he had come up
from the brawling fury of a hundred waterfronts to a command
that he meant to keep.

Jim's eyes narrowed angrily, and his jaw set. Once, he had
deliberately butted in to avert more trouble. Now they were
out to get rid of Jim Mayo as fast as possible.

Carefully, his fingers touched the swollen lump under his
eye and felt his jaw. He felt stiff and sore from the brutal
kicking and beating he'd taken.

Somewhere in the islands, perhaps still back in Makassar,
Major William Arnold was waging an almost single-handed
fight to keep peace in these East Indian waters. But it was a
lonely, dangerous job. All over the world secret agents of the
Gestapo were striking at the lifeline of the British Empire. All
through the islands there was sabotage, propaganda, and undercover warfare.

Slug Brophy came up to the bridge. "Romberg was asking
about you," he said, winking. "When I told him you were on
the bridge, he seemed surprised. Those guys got enough guns
to arm the U.S. Navy."

"Yeah?" Jim stroked his chin thoughtfully. "Let the Gunner
handle this a bit longer. You come with me."

He wheeled and ran down the ladder. Sakim and Longboy
were painting amidships.

"Drop those brushes," Jim snapped. "Slug, get them a couple of guns."

When they were armed he went amidships. The three Germans were sitting in the petty officer's mess, talking and drinking beer. Jim stopped in the doorway.

"I understand," he said crisply, "that you men have guns
aboard. I want them. Nobody packs a rod on this boat but my
officers and myself."

Romberg shrugged. "But in times like this maybe we need our guns," he said softly.

"You get them when you leave the boat," Mayo snapped. "All right, on your feet for a search."

Romberg's face whitened.

Kessler got to his feet, face flushing with anger.

"There will be no searching here!" he snapped. "This is insolence!"

"Yeah?" Ponga Jim chuckled without mirth. "You guys got a lot to learn. An' when you talk about insolence, sourpuss, remember you're not in the German army now. You're on my ship, and I'm in command here!"

Kessler started forward and then stopped. "So? You know, do you? Well, what of it?"

Mayo's gun slid into his hand. "You guys asked for transportation for yourselves and your cargo. You're getting it. Get tough, and you'll get a lot more. I said I'd get you there, but I didn't say I'd get you there alive." He shrugged. "Take their guns, Slug. The first one that peeps will have to digest some lead."

The three men stood very still, hands raised, while Brophy frisked them expertly. Once Romberg's eyes flickered to the port and he stared.

For outside was Sakim, with a rifle barrel resting on the edge. Longboy stood outside the other, his brown face eager.

Romberg's eyes swung back to Mayo, and there was a hint of admiration in them. "You'd have made a good German officer, Captain Mayo."

Jim snorted contemptuously.

Brophy passed out of the room with the guns tucked in his waistband. Then Ponga Jim slid his back into its holster.

"Sorry to have bothered you, gents. Adios."

Day slid into night. Mayo was worried. Something had to break. There was a possibility that disarming them had also wrecked their plans, but he had no faith in the idea. There was something else, something more to be expected. At twelve he would go on watch, and by that time, if everything went well, they would be entering the Banda Sea with a straight shot for Bangkulu before turning east for Banggai Bay.

Night had fallen and the stars were bright when he turned aft for a last look around before his night watch. The passage amidships was empty, but he heard voices in Romberg's cabin.

For an instant, Ponga Jim hesitated outside the door. Kessler was talking. If Braunig was there he was not speaking. But that was usually the case. Jim walked aft to the sternpost and stood watching the wake, his back to the after deckhouse. Then he turned and started forward.

Sharp, fierce snarling and then a shrill, angry yapping shattered the still air. Puzzled, he hesitated. Something was bothering the orangutan. He went down the ladder to the storeroom beneath the after wheelhouse.

In the small space was the cage of the orangutan, a huge beast, almost as big as a gorilla. Foaming at the mouth, the big ape was screaming with fury and trying to get through the bars at Braunig, who was crouching before the cage. His wide, ugly face was contorted with sadistic frenzy as he stabbed at the ape with a pointed stick.

As Ponga Jim reached the foot of the ladder, the ape grabbed the stick and with a terrific jerk, ripped it from Braunig's hands. The stick broke and the ape hurled the pieces at Braunig. The burly German roared with laughter, until one of the sticks hit him on the shoulder. Then, with a snarl of rage, Braunig jerked up a boathook and stabbed at the ape with the sharp end.

"I'll show you!" Braunig snarled. "You slobbering beast!"

Jim crossed the intervening space in a leap, ripping the boathook from Braunig's hands. "I'll be damned if you will!" he snapped. "Get back to your cabin before I lose my temper."

"You! Why, you—!" Braunig's face purpled with fury. *Smack!*

58

Jim's right smashed into the big German's mouth and knocked him skidding along the deck. The German sprang to his feet, crouched, and then lunged. Jim sidestepped.

"Better get on deck before I get peeved," he said again. "I don't want to hurt you."

Braunig was powerful. He wheeled and rushed at Ponga Jim. But Mayo stepped back quickly. The German plowed ahead. Jim crossed a right, hooked both hands to the body, and jerked up a hard right uppercut. Braunig staggered, and Jim knocked him down with a hard left hook. He got up, and Jim floored him again. The big man lay there, groggy, but still conscious.

"All right," Jim said coolly, "now go on deck."

Slowly, heavily, the man climbed to his feet and staggered drunkenly up the ladder. Jim crossed to the cage where the big ape clung to the bars, staring.

"What's the matter, old fellow?" he asked softly. "Been treated pretty mean, haven't you?"

The orangutan stared back at him, its eyes bloodshot, ugly. Staring at the ape, Jim could see that the beast's mind had been warped into a seething caldron of hatred where nothing lived now but the lust to kill. Through the red hair on its body he could see countless scars. Why, Jim wondered? Just cruelty? But why cart the ape around and suffer the expense of keeping it for only cruelty? He shrugged and went up the ladder to the deck.

Brophy was standing in the wing of the bridge when Jim came on watch. "This kind of gets a guy," Brophy said softly. "Something's in the wind, and you don't know what or where it'll come from."

Mayo nodded. "Better get below and turn in," he said. "They won't wait much longer. They've got to strike between here and Banggai, because there's a destroyer there now."

He watched Brophy down to the main deck and then turned back. The visibility was good, for the night was clear and the stars were bright. Tupa, the Alfura seaman taken aboard in Bonthain, was at the wheel, Selim on watch in the bow.

His thoughts reverted to Romberg. There was more in the

wind than a plan to eliminate him. That, he was certain, was only incidental to greater plans, and they must be plans with some bearing on the cargo below. Drilling machinery it might be, and some of it obviously was; but there were other supplies, also.

The sea was calm, just a light wind blowing. He took his glasses and scanned the sea thoughtfully. A sub? There hadn't been a sub sighted since the affair off the New Guinea coast. True, there were German agents in the East Indies; there had been efforts at sabotage, but most of it ineffectual.

Aside from the attempts to create revolt among native tribes in Papua and to destroy shipping, things had gone along smoothly. It was so obvious a tactic to attack the far-flung British Empire at many points, and as Holland was supported by the British navy in the Indies, that included the Netherlands Indies.

Ponga Jim let one hand slip up to the gun butt in the shoulder holster. War couldn't come to the Indies without becoming a personal problem.

Romberg was a wily customer. Had the plot to kill him in the Parakeet Nest succeeded, he would have been safely out of the way, and still the cargo would have gone on to Banggai Bay, and whatever else remained of the plot would have proceeded without further delay.

Sparks walked out on the bridge. "Message for you, Cap," he yawned sleepily. "Just came in."

"Suppose you turn in, Sparks. You may get another long shift tonight. I'll listen in occasionally."

McVey turned and left the bridge. The message was brief and to the point. It said:

NO CARGO EXPECTED BANGGAI. ROMBERG, KESSLER, BRAUNIG UNKNOWN. HAVE YOU GOT YOUR NECK OUT!

WILLIAM.

Ponga Jim frowned thoughtfully. He had suspected that it was some point near Banggai, but that they intended to trans-ship there. He paced the bridge, his mind weighing the possibilities. When Gunner Millan came up to relieve him at four o'clock, he was still far from a solution.

The hours slipped by. The sun came up and the day warmed. The crew was under a strain. The men were jumpy. Several times Jim saw his three passengers gathered in serious conversations, but he ignored them until late in the afternoon. Braunig, his face battered and swollen, had just returned from feeding the orangutan, and the three were standing amidships. Jim came out of the passageway and strolled up to them.

"Suppose you guys let your hair down," he said slowly, "and tell me just where you think you're going? I know it isn't Banggai."

Romberg's lips tightened, and he glanced at Kessler. "Unfortunately, Captain Mayo, our plans have gone somewhat awry. However, it is true we don't have any great desire to land at Banggai. We intended to see the cargo was taken to Tembau."

"My deal says Banggai," Ponga Jim said sharply. "And to Banggai we go."

Romberg cleared his throat. "Captain Mayo, I know something of shipping conditions in these waters now and how difficult it is to keep busy. Suppose I offered you a bonus to carry us to Tembau."

Jim shrugged. "You know my terms: cash first. It'll cost you five thousand. If I don't get it, you go to Banggai and you can deal with the native rajah there." He grinned. "However, he has no love for Germans and is very pro-British."

Romberg hesitated, but Ponga Jim had seen triumph leap into his eyes.

"All right, Captain Mayo," Romberg said. "I'll see you in the salon at dinner. It will take all my available funds and those of my friends. But we'll manage."

On the impulse of the moment, Jim stepped into the radio room when he went forward. Picking up a pencil, he wrote rapidly.

"Tear that up after you send it, Sparks," he ordered. "And stand by."

It read:

WILLIAM GIRARD,
HOTEL KONINGSPLEIN,
MAKASSAR, CELEBES, N. E. I.
 DESTINATION TEMBAU. OUT OF THE FRYING PAN INTO THE FIRE.

MAYO.

The *Semiramis* pushed her bows into the seas, rolling easily on a changed course. Tembau lay on the edge of the Greyhound Strait. There was one anchorage, Ponga Jim Mayo was remembering. It was one he had never seen, but it had become almost a legend in the islands. Tukoh Bay wasn't a nice place, for it had become a resort for all the renegades in the islands. But if it was Tukoh Bay they wanted, to Tukoh Bay they would go.

Tupa was in the crow's nest when the *Semiramis* slipped through the outlying reefs to Tembau. The island lifted itself high out of the water, and from the sea there was no evidence of the village at Tukoh Bay. Slug Brophy came up to the bridge. He had two guns strapped on. Gunner Millan was standing by on the poop deck with several of the crew.

Slowly the old tramp wallowed into Tukoh Bay, and Jim Mayo gave the word to let go forward. A few minutes later, the three Germans went over the side into a native sampan and were taken ashore. Lighters came alongside, and with them, Kessler and Braunig to superintend the discharge of their cargo.

When the last sling was going over the side with its cases, Romberg came aboard.

"Well, Captain, you promised delivery, and here we are. I want to thank you for a pleasant voyage. But as the tide is out, you won't be leaving before daybreak. Perhaps I'll see you before then."

Daybreak! Ponga Jim felt himself turn cold inside. Night in Tukoh Bay? That was something he'd overlooked. The town was full of cutthroats ready for anything that promised payment. He watched the three men go ashore and saw the lighters pull away.

Red Hanlon, the chief engineer, came up from below, wiping his hands. Jim motioned to him.

"Listen, Red, I want you to keep steam up all night. We can't get out of here until daybreak. And with that crowd ashore, anything may happen.

"Tell Slug and the Gunner I want to see them in my cabin, Li, and quick!" Jim ordered the steward.

In a bungalow built back under the trees behind the little village of Tukoh Bay, the three Germans sat together. Behind a low table was another chair, and the man who sat there was thin and bald. He looked old, yet when he moved it was with a grace that proved him much younger than he appeared. His features were narrow, hawklike. A big man, powerfully built, lay on a divan nearby.

The man behind the table shuffled some papers on his desk. "How many men does he have?" he demanded harshly.

"Twenty-five in all," Romberg said. "The steward is a Chinese and can be discounted."

The man behind the desk stared at Romberg coldly. "A Chinese? Discounted? That was what the Japanese thought. Let us not make the same mistake." He paused. "Armament?"

Romberg hesitated. "I'm not sure. Each of the officers is armed. I believe they have two rifles for game, and a shotgun."

"You needn't worry, Herr Heittn," the big man on the divan said. "I've heard a lot of this Ponga Jim Mayo, and those boys of mine would like to take him."

"Don't forget, Petrel," Heittn replied drily, "that a submarine has failed, that this man almost single-handedly captured a ship and destroyed a sub. This man is not to be trifled with. No doubt," he said, glancing at the discoloration on Braunig's eye, "our friend could tell us a little about him."

*   *   *

Heittn glanced from one to the other. "We must not fail this time. The boat must be seized, the crew destroyed."

It was dark in the cabin when Li entered, but he flashed no light. "Captain Mayo?" he whispered. "They come now."

Silently, Ponga Jim got up and strapped on his guns. Then he took down the rifle. By the chronometer, which he struck a match to check, it was almost three in the morning. Another hour and it would be turning gray. He picked up the automatic rifle and walked to the bridge.

Brophy was leaning on the bulwark looking over the dodger. It was pitch dark, but not far out there was a larger blob on the water.

"Tupa in the crow's nest?" Mayo asked.

Brophy nodded. "Yeah, everybody's at his station. What you going to do, Skipper? Hoist 'em aboard with the winches?"

"Wait and see. I'm going to give those boys a bellyful of war."

"I hope you know what you're doing. There's more than two hundred men out there. Selim slipped ashore, and he says they're armed to the whiskers."

The boats were nearer now. Ponga Jim walked back slowly to the wheelhouse.

"All right, Sparks," he commanded. "Lights!"

Suddenly the sea flashed into white brilliance under the rays of three great searchlights, and almost at the same instant, the whistle blew the fire drill signal. Hoses were strung out and connected. The boats swung alongside, and the attackers began swarming up the side.

"*Steam!*" Jim roared, firing a blast into the nearest boat.

In almost the same instant, a roar of steam belched from the fire hoses, full into the faces of the men swarming up the sides and clinging to the rail of the *Semiramis*!

One gigantic half-caste took the blast full in the face at scarcely a yard. His face vanished as if by magic, and screaming

64

horribly, the man let go of the rail and tumbled back into the water.

It was all over in an instant. Screaming in agony, the attackers leaped into the sea. From the bridge, Ponga Jim waited, watching.

Unnoticed, a motor launch had slipped in close to the bow, and suddenly, there was a yell from forward. Ponga Jim spun around, firing as he turned. His shot knocked the gun from the hands of a big Swede he recognized as Hankins.

Then, with a rush, the group swept aft. Two of his own men went down. The others, caught from behind, rushed for shelter aft, unable to handle the hoses effectually without endangering others of the crew. The major attack was broken, but now, with dawn breaking and safety in sight, defeat swept down upon them behind a hail of lead. Jim ran down the ladder, and whirled at the foot of it to find himself face to face with Braunig.

The big German had rushed forward from the after part of the ship, and for an instant Jim failed to appreciate what it might mean. The German jerked up his gun and fired. Mayo dropped into a crouch, hammering a stream of slugs at Braunig. The first shot struck the man in the chest, but by some superhuman burst of strength he lunged forward, firing again.

A terrific blow slammed Mayo on the head, and he spun halfway around, but not before seeing Braunig topple over on his face, dead.

Romberg was nowhere in sight, but the battle had divided itself suddenly into a series of individual scraps. Kessler, leaping from the body of a Malay fireman, his knife red with blood, turned to see Ponga Jim coming toward him. Kessler hurled the knife, but he missed. Then Jim leaped in a flying tackle, and they crashed to the hatch, rolling over and over.

Jim came up on top and leaped free. The German jumped up and landed a left that knocked Jim back on his heels. Kessler let go with another, but Mayo grappled with him and hurled the man back against a winch. As Kessler came at him, Mayo caught him with a short left hook that cracked against the German's chin with a pop like the report of a pistol. Kessler toppled forward, unconscious.

Grabbing up his fallen gun, Ponga Jim ran aft. In the passageway he stumbled over a body. And on number four hatch was another, but the battle seemed to have centered forward. And Jim Mayo could only recall that Braunig had come forward. What could he have done aft? And how did he get there?

Suddenly, a shrill scream of horror sounded from the poop deck, and Mayo reached the stern in two bounds, just in time to see Li come staggering out of the passageway, screaming with fear.

The Chinese steward staggered over a chock and fell headlong just as Jim leaped through the door. He stopped, dead still, feet spread wide.

Not six feet away, the huge orangutan was standing, its bloodshot eyes burning with hate. Its hands, arms, and face were stained with blood, and at its feet lay what was left of Romberg, a horror only to be recognized by the clothing. Then the ape sprang!

Mayo's gun jerked up, and the trigger slammed on an empty chamber. Quickly, Jim dropped the gun and hurled his closed fist at the creature's body. It landed solidly, and the beast gave a queer, gasping cry. Then one hand slapped across Jim's face, knocking him against the bulkhead. The ape sprang, ripping the shirt from his shoulders. But Mayo swung aside, and then leaped, swinging a barrage of blows that knocked the big ape head over heels.

Slowly, the orangutan crawled to its feet. The murderous fury still blazed in its eyes, but it was wary now. This was a different mode of attack, something new. Suddenly, it grabbed the pipes overhead and hurled itself bodily through the air, feet first!

Jim tried to duck, but those feet struck him full in the chest and he turned a complete somersault, sprawling on the deck outside, gasping for breath. The ape sprang at him, snarling and screaming; but Jim rolled over and caught the animal with a vicious kick as it leaped toward him. It toppled back, and Jim smashed a right to the face.

The orangutan dropped to the deck and began to whimper.

Cautiously, Jim got to his feet, and prodded the ape below and into its cage. Then he snapped the lock that Romberg had unfastened. Somehow, the big ape had got to him before he could escape. Trained to hate men and to kill, the beast had acted violently.

Ponga Jim Mayo staggered back to the deck. There were no sounds of fighting now, but when he raised his head he saw a seaplane at anchor nearby. He went toward it.

Major Arnold was leaning against the deckhouse amidships lighting a cigarette. He lifted an eyebrow as he saw how battered Jim was.

"Fighting again?" he asked wearily. "Such brutality! Tsk, tsk, tsk!"

Ponga Jim looked very astonished.

"Me? Fighting? I've done more battling in the last few days than the whole Allied army has done since the war started!"

Arnold nodded. "We got Kessler. What happened to Romberg and Braunig?"

Ponga Jim told him briefly.

"The worst one got away," the major said. "Heittn, his name was. We've been trying to get him for months."

"Have a drink?" Jim invited.

The major nodded. "What were they carrying in those cases, Jim?"

"Ammunition and guns," Jim replied. "It'd have been chaos for us if they'd distributed them. I wasn't certain of their cargo until we reached Tembau. Then I knew."

"Well, here's how," said the major, downing his drink. Then, "Who-o-o-o! What was in that glass?"

"My own concoction. I call it a Barata Sling."

"Gad!" breathed Major Arnold. "What action!"

"Action?" said Ponga Jim Mayo, laughing. "You mean reaction. Wait until you try to get up!"

AUTHOR'S NOTE

QASAVARA

A cannibal spirit and the enemy and rival of Qat, who was the hero-creator of mankind, Qasavara and his House figure in many of the adventure-myths of the New Guinea–Melanesian island area.

Broken Water Bay, so named because of its tricky currents, lies just beyond Cape Wabusi, and near the cape is the mouth of the Sepik River, the largest river in northern New Guinea and one that reaches almost halfway across that island. The Sepik can be navigated up to three hundred miles by vessels drawing up to thirteen feet. Until one reaches Malu there is much lowland, some of it quite marshy, along the banks. Crocodiles are plentiful. None that I glimpsed seemed to be shedding any tears.

Bam Island, mentioned in the story, was an active volcano.

One of my youthful ambitions was to go up the Sepik, cross over the divide, and come down the Fly River. It was an ambition I never attempted to fulfill, which is just as well. The chances of making it at the time were slim, although it would have been interesting to try. It was one of those vague ideas that flutter through the mind of a very young man inclined to wander.

THE HOUSE OF
QASAVARA

Ponga Jim Mayo looked toward the dark blotch of Bam
Island.

"Easy does it," he said, his eyes swinging toward Cape
Wabusi. "Port a little . . . hold it!"

Quickly, Jim Mayo stepped to the *Semiramis*'s engine-room
telegraph and jerked it to stop. They had reached anchorage.

"All right, Mr. Brophy," he called. "Let go forward!"

He stood in the wing of the bridge of the freighter waiting to
hear the splash of the anchor. Then he turned and went down
the ladder.

Carol Sutherland got up quickly when he came into the
ship's salon. His white-topped cap was at a jaunty angle, but
she thought that without the gleam of humor that was never far
from his eyes his bronzed face would have been a little grim.
He had a fighter's jaw, and his broad, powerful shoulders
tapering to a slim waist and narrow hips completed the picture.

"Are we there?" she asked. "Is this Broken Water Bay?"

Ponga Jim nodded. In the glow of the light her red-gold hair
was like a flame.

"Yes, this is it. But you can't go ashore tonight. It will be bad
enough in the daytime."

"But my father's here, and—"

Her protest ended as he lifted a hand. The throb of engines
down below had ceased, but there was another sound, the low,
pulsing beat of drums rolling down from the dark, jungle-clad

71

hills. She stopped, her mouth partly opened to speak, while the sound of the drums filled the room and seemed to pound with the same rhythm as the blood in her veins.

"Hear that?" he asked gravely. "Gets you, doesn't it?" He waited for a moment, listening. "And those fellows are head-hunters or cannibals, Stone Age men living in a land that time forgot. Think of it," he said, waving a hand toward the lonely New Guinea shore. "Most of them have never seen a white man; thousands of them don't know there is such a thing. This is the jungle, Miss Sutherland, jungle as you'll never see it in Africa anymore.

"Back there is a people living in grass huts, using poisoned arrows with barbed heads, painting the skulls of their victims in weird, unbelievable designs. They aren't a proud, noble race like the Polynesians, but people to whom killing is the natural thing. And this is a lonely coast, where few ships come."

"My father is here somewhere, Captain Mayo," she said simply. "I must go to him."

He shrugged. "Okay, lady. If he's ashore, we'll find him tomorrow. No boat leaves this ship before daybreak, I value my men too highly. Those boys ashore are stirred up. This whole country is throbbing with hate. There have been fifty-three natives who worked for white men killed within the past two weeks."

Jim walked into his cabin, and when he returned he wore a gun in his shoulder holster.

"You know," he said thoughtfully, "I can't figure what Colonel Sutherland would be doing on this coast. This Broken Water Bay is an unhealthy country in more ways than one, and certainly no spot for a plantation."

"But I know he came here," she protested. "I heard him mention the bay to this man who came to see him before he left. That man was coming, too. They were to land near the mouth of a small river, and I believe they were going to a village close by."

"That's impossible," he said decidedly. "There isn't any village near here. Those drums are fifteen miles from here at least."

"But I heard them talk about looking for someone, about finding the House of Qasavara."

"The House of Qasavara!" Ponga Jim stuck his thumbs in his belt. "Say, are you kidding me?"

"Why, no," she exclaimed in surprise. "I—"

"But you told me your old man was looking for a plantation location near Broken Water Bay, and now you spring this here Qasavara business on me."

"What's strange about that?" she demanded. "I heard Daddy and this man talking about it, and supposed it was a native village nearby."

Jim tossed his cap on the table and ran his fingers through his hair.

"Listen, baby," he said, exasperated. "Qasavara is a cannibal-spirit living back in that steamy jungle somewhere. The House of Qasavara is where he takes his victims, and where the natives offer sacrifices to him.

"Until a couple of months ago he'd almost been forgotten, then several bodies were found bitten by five poisonous teeth. One was found at Salamoa while we were there, another at Madang, a couple outside of Port Moresby, and one near the airport at Lae. Every one of them was a native employed by white men. Then last week twelve were found at one time, all of them marked by the five teeth of Qasavara."

"But what can all that have to do with Father?" Carol asked. "I don't understand."

Jim shrugged. "You've got me, lady." He rubbed his jaw thoughtfully, and then he looked up, meeting her eyes. "Didn't you tell me your father came from Sydney? That he worked for the government in some inspection service or something?"

"That's right. And about six weeks ago he received a letter from Port Moresby that worried him, and decided to come up here. I came with him, but stopped in Port Moresby."

"How about this guy who came to see him? He was a

73

slender, well-built fellow with a clipped blond mustache, was he? Military walk and all that?"

She nodded, puzzled. "Do you know him?"

"Know him?" Jim chuckled. "He's the best friend I've got. And just so you'll know what you've stumbled into, that father of yours must be in the British Intelligence service!"

After Carol Sutherland returned to her cabin, Ponga Jim walked out on deck. It was completely dark, the sky spangled with stars, but no moon. In the blackness a quarter of a mile away was the darker shoreline and a faint, silver gleam from a rustle of surf.

Jim rubbed his jaw thoughtfully. It would be a joke on Arnold to show up here when Arnold had left him in Menado. And it must be a tough job or Major William Arnold would never have sent to Colonel Sutherland for assistance in breaking the case.

Yet he had seen in the few ports he had touched that the natives were frightened and surly. Whispers had come to him that all whites were to be murdered, and all those who worked for whites; that Qasavara had returned to claim Papua and would kill all Dutch and British people.

There was a stirring of unrest throughout the islands, and an outbreak now, calling for ships, money, and men, would be a severe blow to England. Besides, the Indies were the richest prize on earth, and to countries thirsting for colonies and expansion, they represented a golden opportunity.

Several times, Ponga Jim and Major William Arnold had spiked the guns of the Gestapo and other foreign agents working in the Indies. But those had been attempts at sinking ships and at destroying commerce in the islands. The present effort would stir up much more strife than the former attempts.

Then he looked up and saw the head.

A native, his face frightfully painted with streaks of white, was crawling over the rail. Even as Ponga Jim's eyes caught the movement, a dozen other bodies lifted into view and the rail was swarming with savages. Jim let out a yell and went for his gun.

At the first blast of fire three heads vanished. Another native, already on the deck, let out a wild yell and pitched over on his face. With a scream of rage a big savage hurled a spear that missed by an eyelash and then, jerking a stone hatchet from his belt, hurled himself at Jim, his face twisted with hatred.

Dropping into a crouch that sent the wild blow with the hatchet over his shoulder, Jim whipped a terrific left hook to the Papuan's belly. Then he jerked erect and slammed the man alongside the head with a wicked, chopping blow from the barrel of his automatic. Without a sound the native dropped to the deck.

From the bridge a machine gun broke into a choking roar that whined into an angry snarl as burst after burst swept the rail and the boats thronging out from shore. Jim snapped a quick shot at a big headhunter running aft, and wheeled around to see Selim wrest a spear from another and run him through.

Abo, one of the seamen, was down on the deck, writhing with agony, but Tupa had jumped astride his murderer's shoulders from the boat deck and buried a knife in the man's neck.

As swiftly as they had come, they were gone, and the rail was littered with bodies. Jim ran to the taffrail and snapped a couple of quick shots at the boats. He was rewarded by seeing one native jerk to his feet and topple over the side.

Slug Brophy came running aft with Red Hanlon and two of the crew. All carried rifles.

"Take 'em, boys!" Slug roared. "Let 'em have it!"

The rifles crashed, and volley after volley smashed into the fleeing boats. One of them swung broadside, drifting helplessly with the tide, its cargo only death.

"That'll hold them," Jim said drily. "I wonder what started that?"

Slug grinned. "You can't chase all over the ocean mixing into trouble wherever you find it without getting guys after your scalp!" he said grimly. "These babies didn't tackle this boat because they wanted, but because they were told to!"

"Yeah," Jim agreed. "You got something there."

Suddenly he thought of Carol and started forward on a run. He swung into the starboard passage and stopped dead still.

At the end of the passage her door swung idly with the slight roll of the ship, and the room beyond was lighted and empty. In the passage, a native woman lay on the floor, dead.

Jim swore viciously and leaped over the sprawled body. One glance told him that Carol was gone. Wheeling, he saw another native huddled in a corner, run through with his own spear. A groan startled him.

Whirling, gun in hand, he saw Longboy struggling to sit up, blood running from a gash on his scalp. Quickly, he knelt beside him.

"What was it, Boy?" he asked. "What happened?"

"Six, eight mans, they come overside while you fight. I see them. I hit one, knock him over. I throw marlinespike, get another one. Then pretty soon I in here, mans grab Missee, I sock 'em. Stick him with spear. Somebody shoot—bang, I no know what happen."

Jim got to his feet. "Red, get this man to the steward, you hear? Slug, we're going ashore. Those babies can't travel much faster than we can. I brought that dame down here, and I'll see she gets to her old man in one piece. Gunner stays here in charge. I'll take you, Selim, Tupa, Abdul, the Strangler, and Hassan. We've got to move fast!"

When the boat touched the sand the moon was just lifting over the horizon. Jim Mayo shifted his rifle to his left hand.

"Red, you and Fly Johnny take the boat back," he ordered. "I'll keep Singo and Macabi with the rest of us. We might stumble into a tough scrap. Tell the Gunner to get the hook up if I'm not back by daylight and take her around to the Sepik. If we don't get them we'll pick you up about two miles up off Sago Bar."

Turning quickly, he struck off at a rapid walk. The natives would be traveling fast, as they would not expect pursuit before daylight and there was little chance of an ambush near the bay. Giant ficus trees spread their aerial roots beside the path, and there was heavy undergrowth, mostly ferns and sugarcane. The jungle shut in suddenly, dark and ominous.

Ponga Jim slowed his pace. Just how many men were in the band ahead he could not guess. Probably forty or fifty, for there had been nearly a hundred in the attacking party, and fearful execution had taken place along the rail and in some of the boats.

Slug hurried up alongside Jim. His short, powerful body moved as easily and rapidly as any one of the long, lithe seamen behind. "Gosh, Skipper, I hate to think of them Guineas having Miss Sutherland. That girl was a bit of all right."

"Yeah," Jim nodded gravely. "You bet she was. But I'm not worried about them. That attack was planned by a white man for a purpose. You know what I think, Slug? Somebody knew that girl was aboard!"

"You mean they jumped us just to get her?"

"That's just what I mean. At first, I thought it was some of the same bunch we've had trouble with, and they recognized the boat. I thought maybe they were afraid we were going to butt in again. But now I think they had some spy who saw the girl come aboard in Port Moresby or saw her at Salamoa. The attack was a blind so that, under cover, they could get her."

"But what's the idea? What good would she be to them?"

"None, unless—" Jim hesitated, frowning.

"Unless what?"

"Unless they've got her father, and probably Arnold. They could use her to put pressure on Sutherland and Arnold, to make them give up a lot of information that both of them have. Those two are the big boys of the counterespionage movement down here. They know all the ropes."

Slug hitched his gun a little and swore under his breath. He knew only too well what fiendish tortures those savages could think of, but it wasn't the Papuans who would be worst, for the civilized men who led them would be most dangerous.

In the damp light of dawn they stopped for a hurried lunch. All the men were silent, grim. Jim scouted out along the trail with Tupa. Tupa knelt in the mud, pointing.

"See? They come this way," he said.

Jim studied the marks of high heels thoughtfully. Several times during the night his flashlight had picked them out along the trail among the tracks of other men. Now, in the growing light of day, they were plainer.

Ponga Jim swore suddenly.

"Slug!" he called. Brophy came running. "Look at those tracks! Carol Sutherland never made those! She'll weigh about a hundred and fifteen, and by now she'd be tired. Yet those steps are light. They've got a child or a Negrito wearing those shoes!"

Brophy scowled. "But where the hell—"

"The river!" Jim said suddenly. "They made for the river. Get that stuff out of the way and let's go!"

In a matter of minutes the packs were made, and Ponga Jim led off into the jungle at a rapid walk. As he walked, his mind worked rapidly. It could be either Heittn or Petrel, but somehow he believed this last attack was by someone new to him.

William, not so long since, had mentioned something about two German agents, Blucher and Kull, who had come into the Indies. Despite the loneliness of some sections of the New Guinea coast, it would be a poor place from which to operate. His common sense told him that the seat of the trouble would be in the dark and little-known interior. Legends placed the House of Qasavara somewhere in the unknown country at the headwaters of the Sepik.

They were following a well-beaten trail, and Jim paused from time to time to listen, but heard no sound. He was sure the trail would bring him out somewhere near Sago Bar, where he could intercept the *Semiramis*. Despite time and trouble, regardless of danger, it was up to him to follow the natives who had captured Carol Sutherland. Also, there was a chance Arnold was somewhere up the river and in terrible danger.

Dawn was just breaking when they came out on the bank of the river. About a mile wide, it rolled rapidly seaward, bearing here and there a giant tree or snag floated from the jungle upriver. The flood season was past, but the water was still high. The Sepik would carry a boat that didn't draw more than thirteen feet for at least three hundred miles. With a good deal of extra water, there was a chance he could go much farther than that.

Tupa glided to his side, moving soundlessly.

"Papua boy, he come!" he whispered, pointing up the bank.

Moving toward him in the early light of dawn he saw a dozen powerful savages.

"Wussi River boy," Tupa said softly. "They bad. Plenty mean."

The Wussi River was some distance west, and these boys were far off their usual beat. Ponga Jim shifted his rifle to the hollow of his arm and waited. His dealings with the natives there had been friendly, but for the most part they were a surly bunch. Many of them understood a few words of German and called small coins "marks." Obviously, a remnant of the touch of civilization acquired when the Germans had owned that section, prior to the world war.

Jim stepped forward. "You see Papua boy? White girl?"

The Wussi River men stared at him sullenly, muttering among themselves, but did not reply. Then one of them, a big man, stepped from the crowd and began a fierce harangue. His voice rose and fell angrily, and he made fierce gestures. Ponga Jim watched him warily.

"What's he say, Tupa?" he asked guardedly.

"He say you go away. You bad white man. Qasavara very angry. Pretty soon he call all white men, all who know or talk to white men. Mebbe so all people who no fight white men."

"Tell him that's a lot of hooey," Jim said coolly. "Tell him I'm a friend, that all Englishmen are his friends, too. Tell him Qasavara is dead, he was killed by Qat, the good spirit."

Tupa told him quickly, but the native shook his head stubbornly. Tupa's eyes widened.

"He say Qasavara has many men. Pretty soon he kill all English. He say Qasavara has dragons, two of them, with wings. Pretty soon take plenty heads."

"Yeah?" Jim said. He hooked his thumbs in his belt. "So they got some ships? You tell that monkey face I personally will take care of Qasavara. Tell him he swiped my woman."

Jim grinned and shifted the gun in his hands, watching the natives warily.

"Hey, Skipper!" Brophy said suddenly. "Here comes some more from the other direction! About twenty of them!"

Ponga Jim wheeled, but as he turned, he caught a flicker of movement from the jungle trail along which they had come. More headhunters.

"All right, boys," he said casually. "We're in for a fight. But we always win our fights, so take it easy and back up to those snags on the bar. Brophy, you and the Strangler get over there behind those logs now. Just walk over, taking it easy. As soon as you get sheltered, cover our retreat. Get me?"

"Right down the groove, Skipper!" Brophy said cheerfully.

"Selim! Abdul! Hassan!" Jim snapped quickly. "Take that downriver bunch. Tupa, watch the jungle. You too, Singo. Macabi, you follow Brophy back to those snags."

He had noticed the snags before they were scarcely on the bank of the river. A half dozen giant jungle trees of the ficus type had floated here and beached themselves on Sago Bar. Tumbled together, they formed a rude semicircle facing the jungle, open toward the river. They presented a natural fortress from four to six feet high.

"All right, Tupa," he said finally, "you tell that big walrus we're going out on the bar to cook some breakfast."

The big man spoke suddenly, fiercely, walking rapidly toward them. Tupa looked worried.

"He say you move, he kill!" he said.

"Yeah?" Jim grinned. He handed his rifle to Tupa. "All right, when I sock this lug, you guys leg it back on that bar. Get sheltered as quick as you can, see?" The big native, a powerful man with huge muscles and an ugly face, came closer. "Watch it, Brophy!" Jim said loudly. "Here comes the fireworks!"

The big native stepped close and grabbed at Jim's arm. Then Jim hit him a short, wicked right chop that laid the man's cheek open for four inches. A short left hook came up into the man's belly, and the savage pitched forward on his face. A howl of anger went up, and suddenly, they rushed.

Ponga Jim whipped out his automatic and fired rapidly as he backed up. Two natives spilled over on their faces, and then the rifles behind him began to crash. He turned and legged it for shelter. Something caught at his sleeve, but it wasn't until he was safe behind the log that he looked down. Slug's face was pale.

An arrow had gone through his sleeve near the wrist. One of those ugly, barbed arrows typical of the Papuans. Jim drew it out carefully.

"Would you look at that?" he said. "A yard long and six sharp bits of bone stuck in the shaft. If that got in a man they'd have to cut a six-inch hole to get it out. And those things are steeped in decayed meat. Starts septic poisoning." He tossed the arrow over the log. "Let that be a lesson to you guys. Don't any of you get hit."

Five of the natives were stretched out on the river bank, and the rest had drawn back to the edge of the woods. There were at least a hundred savages inside the edge of that jungle by now, not over seventy yards away. Jim sat down and reloaded the clip in his automatic.

"You guys watch your step now," he said cheerfully. "There's nine rifles here and if we can't keep those guys from crossing that beach, we're a bunch of saps. Those boys can fight, but they haven't any belly for this stuff. If they start to come out, wait until nine of them are in sight. Then let them have it."

*　　*　　*

81

Slug touched Jim on the shoulder. "What did you hit that guy with?" he asked. "He hasn't wiggled a toe yet!"

"Hell, no!" Jim looked disgusted. "I hit that guy with my Sunday punch, and if he ever moves again, he's lucky. But I hit his cheek, not his chin, so he'll probably be able to crawl away in a few minutes."

"Here they come!" Slug said suddenly, and Ponga Jim whirled to see a wave of savages break from the edge of the jungle. Coolly, carefully, his men began to fire, and the brown line wilted like wheat before a mowing machine.

The attack broke, and the remaining natives fled, with at least thirty men scattered on the beach.

"Now what do they think of Qasavara?" Ponga Jim muttered drily. "Get set, you guys! Here comes the *Semiramis!*"

The freighter was steaming up the river, and slowly the bow swung over in the channel, and a boat was lowered. On top of the chart house, Red Hanlon suddenly appeared and jerked the canvas jacket off the machine gun. He sat down behind it, and suddenly the gun began to rattle, drawing a thin line of steel along the jungle.

Red Hanlon met Jim at the rail as he came up the pilot ladder.

"We got a guy here says he knows right where the House of Qasavara is," he said.

Ponga Jim turned and looked at the powerful young native. Big, stalwart, and beautifully muscled, he carried a spear and a large knife in a wooden sheath. His head was shaven in front. Jim frowned.

"You're no Papuan," he said. "You're a Toradjas boy."

The big native nodded eagerly. "Me Toradjas. Me go Celebes, Banggai, Balabac, Zamboanga. Pretty soon me come Salamoa, come here."

"You get around, don't you?" Jim said, speculatively. "You know where the House of Qasavara is?"

"Me sabby. These boy," the Toradjas made a careless gesture that took in all Papua, "they afraid Qasavara. I see his

82

house close by Ambunti. Five white man there, one hifty-hifty. Two white man tie up. One you friend."

"My friend?" Jim said, incredulously. "What makes you think so?"

"Me see you him Amurang one time. You go Qasavara?"

"Yeah," Jim said. "What do you call yourself?"

"Man in Makassar, he call me Oolyssus," he said proudly. "Now Lyssy."

"Ulysses?" Jim grinned. "Not far wrong at that, boy. You get around. All right, let's go!"

All day they steamed steadily up the Sepik. Here and there a cloud of herons flew up, or a flock of wild pigeons. Along the muddy banks crocodiles sunned themselves, great, ugly-looking fellows, many times larger than any seen downstream.

"What's the plan, Skipper?" Slug said, walking up from the main deck at eight bells.

Jim shrugged. "No plan. Ambunti is two hundred and sixty miles from the mouth. It will be nearly morning before we get there. I'm going to take Lyssy and go out to that House of Qasavara, and what happens after that will be whatever looks good."

"You're not leaving me, Skipper. There's going to be a mess back in those woods, and you know it. You can just figure Brophy in on that, or I quit!"

"Okay, Slug," Jim said. "I can use you. I think this Toradjas is on the level. Good men, those fellows, good seamen, fierce fighters, and they don't have a bit of use for other natives. Think they are superior. I've seen a lot of them, and they are all loyal, and they'd tackle their weight in mountain lions."

It was pitch dark when they dropped the anchor in the shelter of a river bend near Ambunti. The current was slack there, and the water sounded three fathoms. Silently, a boat was lowered, settling into the water with only a slight splash. Then the three men rowed ashore and slipped into the brush.

Ponga Jim stumbled along the path in the dark, following

Lyssy and with Brophy bringing up the rear. They had made something more than two miles when suddenly Lyssy stopped dead still. In the same instant, a light flashed in Jim's eyes, and before he could move, a terrific blow crashed down over his head. He felt himself sinking as a wave of blinding pain swept over him, and he desperately tried to regain his feet. Then there was another blow, and he slid to his face in the muddy trail.

It was a long time later when he came to. His lids fluttered open, but he lay still, without trying to move, but trying desperately to understand where he was. He realized suddenly that he was lying face down on a stone floor. He twisted, and an agonizing pain struck him like a blow. He turned over slowly.

"Ah!" said a voice sarcastically. "The sleeping beauty awakens!"

He struggled to sit up, but was bound hand and foot. Still, after a struggle, he managed it. Slowly, he glanced around.

"Well, well! What a pretty bunch this is!" he muttered.

Major William Arnold sat opposite him, his face dirty and unshaven. Beside him was Colonel Sutherland, a plump man with a round British face and calm blue eyes. Further away along the wall was Carol herself, her clothes torn, her face without makeup, but looking surprisingly attractive.

"William," Ponga Jim said slowly. "I never thought I'd see the time when I'd see you wrapped up like that."

There was a groan, and he turned slightly to see Slug Brophy coming out of it.

"You too, eh? What happened to our Toradjas?"

"He got away," Slug grunted. "That guy has skin like an eel. They grabbed him, and then he was gone—just like that."

"Now what?" Carol said brightly. "All you brave and bold he-men should be able to get out of a little mess like this."

"I don't think you can depend on them, Miss Sutherland," a cool voice said in very precise English.

Jim turned his head stiffly and saw two men standing in the door. One was a thick, broad-shouldered man with a powerful neck and the arms of an ape. The other man was tall, obviously a man of some culture.

"Permit me, Captain Mayo," he said with exaggerated politeness. "My coworker, Wilhelm Blucher. I am Count Franz Kull."

As he spoke, two more men appeared in the door.

"Ah, yes! And this is Fritz Heittn, with whose brother you have already come in contact, and this," he indicated the tall, very dark man with massive, stooped shoulders, "is Torq Vokeo. You will know him well, very well, no doubt!"

"He must be the one Lyssy said was hifty-hifty," Jim said sarcastically. "I'd lay you five to one that if he's got an ounce of white blood it's yellow!"

The man's nostrils flared, and over his face swept a sort of fiendish rage that transformed him suddenly into a monster capable of any inhuman cruelty. Kull caught Vokeo's arm.

"Not now," he said gently, smiling faintly. "Wait. We will give you plenty of time for Captain Mayo later.

"You know, Captain," he warned, "Vokeo is our expert in the matter of helping people to remember—you understand? He is, I might add, very efficient."

He turned abruptly. "No more of this horseplay. Major Arnold, you will give me copies of the codes I asked for at once. You will also tell me where your other men are located and what their tasks are. I want that information by noon tomorrow. If I do not have it then, Miss Sutherland will be tortured until you give it to us. I should dislike to leave her to the tender mercies of Torq, but that is a matter for you and her father to decide."

He looked down at Ponga Jim coldly. "As for you, Captain Mayo, there can be only one answer—death. We can't have you in our way further. Within twenty-four hours our bands of native warriors will strike Salamoa, Lae, Madang, Hollandia, and elsewhere. Two of our planes will bomb Port Moresby, and within a matter of hours, New Guinea will be in our complete possession. Nevertheless, I shall deem it a great privilege to have the honor of wiping you off the slate. You've given us no end of trouble."

"Yeah?" Jim grinned insultingly. "And that isn't the half of it, Herr Kull. I'm going to give you a lot more. Do you think I came up here without reporting what I knew? You haven't a chance!"

Kull laughed. "We'll see about that! As for reporting what you knew, we had you under espionage until you were on the river. There has been no chance since then."

Turning, he motioned to the others. "We'll give them a little time to think matters over. Then you may have them, Torq."

When the heavy door closed and locked, Ponga Jim shrugged.

"Nice people!" he said expressively. "But if he thinks I'm going to lie here and wait, he's got another guess coming."

Just then the door opened softly, and Torq Vokeo stepped in. He held an iron spit, its end red-hot and glowing. He smiled at Jim, baring his teeth wolfishly.

"You think is funny, eh? I show you!"

Quickly, Vokeo stepped across the room.

"Get set, Slug!" Jim said suddenly.

Throwing himself on his back, he kicked out viciously with his bound legs. Vokeo, caught with a terrific kick on the upper legs, stumbled and fell headlong. Instantly, Slug Brophy rolled over on top of the man.

Arnold, his eyes suddenly gleaming with hope, rolled over quickly three times, and rolled across Torq's legs. Then Sutherland rolled on his head. Cursing viciously, his oaths muffled by Sutherland's weight, Torq struggled to get free, but the three heavy bodies were too much for him.

Even as the man fell, Jim rolled over and pushed his tied wrists against the red hot spit. The smell of burning hemp filled the room. Time and again his wrists wavered, and burned him, but he persisted. Then, suddenly, he gave a terrific jerk, swelling his muscles with all his great strength. Slowly then, the rope stretched; another jerk, and it came apart!

With a leap, he was on his feet, and in a matter of seconds, he had untied Arnold. Then, as Arnold bent over Brophy's wrists, Jim grabbed Torq by the throat to stifle his shouts, and calmly slugged him on the chin. Then, while Arnold and Brophy freed Sutherland and his daughter, Ponga Jim bound the unconscious man and gagged him.

"Only one gun," Jim said, getting up. "You take it, Colonel. I'll have me another in a minute."

He walked directly to the door and without a second's hesitation, pulled it open. The native guard turned, and Ponga Jim's fist met him halfway. Coolly, Jim dragged him inside, smacked him again, and then passed his rifle to Arnold and his knife to Slug.

"What about you?" Carol asked, wide-eyed.

Major Arnold smiled wryly. "You ask that after seeing him use his hands? When Jim Mayo goes into action he doesn't want anything in the way."

Ponga Jim grinned. "Folks, it might be a good idea to wait here until they come back again, but I'm no hand to wait. Personally, I say we move right now. We make a break for the open, and once there, if attacked, it is every man—and woman— for himself. Make for the river at the big bend below. Ambunti. That's where the ship is."

He jerked open the door, and they started walking, fast. They had reached the end of a long, low stone hall before they were seen. A native guard half turned. Then he opened his mouth to scream. Jim sprang, but too late. A ringing yell awoke a million echoes in the hall. Then Jim slugged him.

But the native was big, and he was tough. With a yell of savage fury, he lurched to his feet and dove for Jim's legs. Jim tried to sidestep and then fell headlong.

"Run, damn you!" he yelled at the others.

Then he jerked to a sitting position and hooked a short left to the native's eye. It jarred the man loose, and Jim lurched to his

feet and kicked him viciously in the stomach. With a howl of
pain, the man rolled over on the floor.

In the yard outside there was a rattle of gunfire. And suddenly Fritz Heittn stepped into sight with a submachine gun.
His eyes narrowed with eagerness as he saw the group clus-
tered just beyond the door, and he lifted the gun. Then he saw
Ponga Jim.

Concealed by a bend in the stair, Jim was slipping quickly
and silently up the stairs. A dozen steps away when Heittn saw
him, Jim leaped to his feet and lunged, even as Heittn brought
the machine gun down and pulled on both triggers!

But suddenly, even as Jim staggered erect, the gun slipped
by him and went plunging down the stair. At the top of it,
Fritz Heittn stood dead still, his eyes wide and staring. Then
slowly, he leaned forward and fell face down on the steps.
Sticking from between his shoulder blades was the haft of a big
knife!

Startled, Jim stared along the stone platform where Heittn
had stood. Coming toward him, at a rapid trot, was Lyssy.
Grinning, he stooped over and retrieved his knife.

With a quick slap on the Toradjas's shoulder, Ponga Jim ran
down the steep steps and grabbed up the fallen machine gun.
Then he stepped to the door. Across the narrow landing field
he could see Arnold and Brophy disappearing into the woods
after the others. Following them were Blucher and a dozen
renegades.

Ponga Jim took in the situation at a glance. The two planes,
one a heavy bomber, the other a small amphibian, were not a
hundred yards away. Without a second's hesitation, Jim made
his decision. He started down the landing field, which was
actually a wide stone terrace belonging to the temple of Qasavara,
toward the planes. A bullet whizzed by his ear from behind
and smacked viciously against the stones ahead of him. Wheeling around, Jim caught sight of two figures silhouetted against
the sky on the temple roof. He swept the machine gun to his

shoulder, fired a burst, and saw one of the men fall headfirst over the parapet and take a long plunge to the stone terrace below. The other man vanished.

Jim wheeled, and as he turned a gun crashed, almost in his ear it seemed, and a bullet smashed into the machine gun and glanced off, ripping a gash in his sleeve and tearing a ragged cut along his arm. Franz Kull was standing not ten feet away, a Luger aimed at Ponga Jim's stomach. The gun was pointed and the finger tightening on the trigger, and there wasn't a chance in the world of him missing at that distance.

Jim staggered, and slowly his knees buckled. He tumbled over on his face. Kull hesitated, lowering the Luger to cover Ponga Jim's still form.

"Got him," Kull whispered. "They got him after all!"

He glanced quickly around. Blucher was furiously directing his band of renegades in the pursuit of the escaped prisoners.

Kull smiled and slipped the gun into his waistband. He stood for a minute, staring down at Ponga Jim Mayo's body, at the slow pool of blood gathering under his left side.

"Almost," he said, "I am sorry."

He stooped and caught Jim by the arm, turning him over. He saw Jim's eyes flicker open and saw the right fist start, and in one panic-stricken moment, realized he had been tricked. Then that fist slammed against the angle of his jaw, and he staggered, grabbing for his gun.

Like a tiger, Jim was on his feet. A left knocked the gun from Kull's hand, and a right sent him reeling against the parked bomber. But Kull was not one of Europe's crack amateur heavyweights for nothing. He straightened, slipped Ponga Jim's left, and hooked a hard left to the head. He ducked a right, and sunk a left in Jim's body, then a right.

Ponga Jim grinned. "A boxer, eh?" he said.

He jabbed quickly, and the punch set Kull off balance. A right caught him in the midsection, and a sweeping left sent him to his knees. Coolly, Jim stepped back.

"Get up, Kull, and take a socking!" he ordered.

Kull straightened and then rushed, hooking hard with both

hands. Jim staggered, grinned, and tied Kull up, whipping a wicked left to his head and body. The punches traveled scarcely six inches, yet they landed with sledgehammer force. Kull jerked away, and Mayo whipped up a right uppercut that knocked him back against the plane. Then Jim stepped in and crossed a short, hard right. Kull slipped to the stone pavement.

Ponga Jim wheeled and swung open the door to the cabin of the amphibian.

The motor sputtered and then roared into life. Out of the corner of his eye, Jim saw Blucher turn, puzzled. Then he started, and gave her the gun. It was little room for a takeoff, but enough, and Ponga Jim cleared the trees at the other end of the terrace by a matter of inches. He zoomed for altitude and then banked steeply and came back flying low.

Blucher stared at him, puzzled, and a half dozen of the renegades stared upward. Then Jim cut loose with both machine guns, raking the terrace.

With a roar of rage, Blucher jerked up his gun, but the blast of leaden death was too much for him, and he broke and ran for the jungle. His men were less fortunate, and the machine guns swept the terrace like a bolt of lightning.

Then it was all over. Slowly he wheeled above the huge stone building, getting a good look at it for the first time, the great towers, the battlements, and the queer, fantastic architecture. Jim glanced over the side, and nothing moved on the terrace.

He turned the plane and flew for the distant masts of the *Semiramis*.

Night had fallen when they met on the Captain's deck of the tramp freighter. Above on the bridge, Slug Brophy paced casually, watching the channel as the dark jungle-clad banks slid by.

Ponga Jim leaned back in his deck chair, pushing back his cap.

"There goes your Qasavara trouble, William!" he said cheerfully. "Again Mayo comes to the rescue. It seems I have to save the British Empire about once every thirty days."

Arnold chuckled. "You aren't doing so bad. Picked up a nice amphibian plane, just like that."

"The fortunes of war, William, merely the fortunes of war! Hello! Here comes Ulysses!"

The big Toradjas stopped a few feet away and then stepped forward, handing Ponga Jim a thick wad of Bank of England notes. Colonel Sutherland gulped, and his eyes widened. "Me find him House of Qasavara," he said. "You take, eh?"

"You bet I'll take!" Jim said, winking at Arnold. "Ah, the sinews of war! Ulysses, you are now a member of my crew, a full-fledged member!"

"You betcha!" Ulysses said.

"That man," Major Arnold said positively, "has the makings of either a thief or a philosopher!"

Ponga Jim got up and offered his arm to Carol.

"Both, William, both! He's going to be a soldier of fortune!"

AUTHOR'S NOTE

HALMAHERA

Halmahera is a smaller version of the spiderlike Celebes, one of the famed Spice Islands that drew ships from all the world. Wild bananas still grow there, and when ripe they split open exposing a thick mass of black seeds. The banana is one of the oldest, if not the oldest, domesticated fruit, probably as old on the earth as man himself. In its several forms, it has long been a staple of his diet.

Gam Konora, mentioned in the story, was the only active volcano on Halmahera, although the interior of the island is mountainous and rugged. Few people live in the interior, dwelling instead along the coast where the sea offers a rich harvest.

At the time of which I write there was a constant cloud of smoke hanging above the crater of Gam Konora.

Indonesia has more than its share of strange and interesting lakes. On the island of Flores are the colored lakes of Gelimoetoe, one a deep jade green, one a perfect blue, the last a deep red. These are crater lakes, and the saying is that when people die they go to the lakes, the young to the green lake, the old to the blue, and the evil to the red lake.

Not far from them is the country of the dragon lizards of Komodo. These are largely found on the island of Komodo, close by, but also on Flores itself. These lizards often weigh several hundred pounds and for short distances can run fast enough to overtake a horse. They are meat eaters and can be very fierce. They will stand up on their hind legs and tail to survey the country around.

WELL OF THE
UNHOLY LIGHT

Rain had fallen for three days, and the jungle dripped with it. The fourth day had begun with heavy showers and faded into a dense fog. Yet despite the rain, the drums had not stopped.

The path was a slide of mud between two solid walls of jungle, green by day, an impenetrable blackness by night. Three miles by trail, they had said. It would be like Frazer to live in such a place. He walked slowly. The drums bothered him.

He knew as much about the interior of Halmahera as anyone did, which wasn't a great deal. Mostly, the natives lived along the coast, rarely going into the interior. But the drums were somewhere beyond Mount Sahu, apparently, and they might be as far away as Gam Konora.

The only way he could tell when he reached the clearing was by the sudden feeling of space around him. Then he glimpsed a light from the bungalow. He wondered again why Frazer had sent for him. The man had never been one to ask for help. He had been notoriously a lone wolf.

Suddenly he dropped to a crouch and then squatted down, listening. Someone was coming around the house! He dropped one hand to the gravel path to balance himself and waited. The footsteps stopped abruptly, and he realized the person had stepped off the path. He heard then the soft swish of receding steps through the grass. He started to call out, but then thought better of it and waited.

After a moment, he stepped up on the veranda and rapped softly. There was no reply. He pushed the door open and stepped in.

Then he stopped. The headless body of a man lay on the floor beside the desk! Staring, he stepped closer, noticing an old tattoo on the hand, between the forefinger and thumb. A faded blue anchor. Stepping carefully around the pool of blood, he glanced at the papers on the desk. He was just reaching to pick them up when a cold voice interrupted:

"So, we have a murderer!" The man's voice was flat. "Put your hands up."

Looking up he saw three men standing in the doorway. The speaker was a tall man with a cold white face, blue eyes, and blond hair. The others were obviously policemen.

"I'm afraid you've made a wrong guess," he said, smiling. "I came to pay Bent Frazer a visit and found things like this."

"Yes?" The man was icily skeptical. "Nevertheless, you will consider yourself under arrest. It so happens that Benton Frazer had no visitors. He was a recluse."

"You think I murdered this man?"

"What else am I to think when I find you standing over the body with bloody hands?"

Involuntarily, he glanced down. His right hand *was* bloody!

But mingled with the blood sticking to his hand were tiny bits of sand and gravel. The path, that was it! When he crouched he had put his hand down. Whoever had carried the head away had obviously gone that way or else was wounded himself. Then, he thought swiftly, the man he had heard had not been the murderer, unless he had returned on a second trip!

"Don't be dumb," he said sharply. "If I killed him, where's the head?"

The man scowled. "You could have disposed of that. Hans," he snapped, "keep an eye on the prisoner. Thomsen, you will search the house!" He turned to the prisoner. "I am Karl

Albran, the resident official from Susupu. Now what is your name, and where are you from?"

"My name?" the prisoner echoed. "My name is Mayo—Ponga Jim Mayo. I'm skipper of the freighter *Semiramis*, of Gorontalo."

"Ponga Jim Mayo!" Albran's face blanched. Then slowly the expression faded, to be replaced with something like triumph. "So," he said softly, "Ponga Jim Mayo! I have heard of you, my friend." Albran turned slightly. "Hans, this fellow has made something of a record for escaping from tight corners. So shoot if he makes even one false move."

Hans smiled wolfishly. "This is one corner he won't get out of!" he said. "I hope he tries."

After Albran turned on his heel and left the room, Jim let his eyes rove around. There was still the problem of the murdered man. To the right of him, and near the window, was a pool of water. Remembering his own movements, he recalled that he had come around the other side of the blood, and none of the three recent arrivals had stood over there. Then, naturally, it had been someone else, who had arrived on the scene and surveyed it carefully and without interruption. Probably the man who had stepped from the path. But who?

A white man, Jim was sure. Bare feet don't make such a sound on a gravel path. And white men in Halmahera were few and all too easily traced. Albran? He considered that. Yet it was hardly probable. And why had the head been removed?

Albran and Thomsen returned to the room with two other men. One of them Jim recognized instantly as Doc Fife. The roving surgeon was known in all the islands. He glanced at Jim out of shrewd eyes.

"Albran tells me you killed Frazer," said Fife, smiling a little. "I told him he was crazy."

Jim shrugged, said nothing.

Albran's eyes were cold. "I found him here, starting to go through the papers on the desk. The body was still warm, and Jim had blood on his hand. Has it now. And I say he killed Frazer!"

97

Ponga Jim stared at Albran very thoughtfully. "Want a case pretty bad, don't you?" he said.

Albran smiled coldly. "This is time of war. I shall not delay the progress of justice, but order you shot—immediately."

"What?" Fife demanded angrily. "Why, you can't do that, Albran! Nothing has been proved—"

"Proved?" Albran demanded. "Am I to deny the sight of my eyes?"

"Wait a minute!" Jim snapped. "I'm getting sick of this nonsense! If the sight of your eyes was worth anything you'd know the dead man is not Bent Frazer!"

Albran whirled, consternation in his eyes. Fife looked startled.

"What do you mean?" Albran demanded.

"Notice the faded blue anchor tattooed on the man's hand?" Jim said drily. "Frazer wouldn't let himself be tattooed under any circumstances. Then, he was at least two inches taller than this man and not so heavily built. This is Kimberly Rinehart. He was a friend of Frazer's. I knew him well and recognized the body as soon as I came in."

"Then—then where's Frazer?" Albran exclaimed. "He must have murdered this man!"

"Nuts," Jim said drily. "Frazer wouldn't kill Rinehart. He is one of the few friends Frazer ever had. In fact, I think whoever killed this man thought he was killing Frazer. I think somebody wanted Bent Frazer dead. They sent a man to kill him, and he killed the wrong man."

"Perhaps you know more about that than we do!" Albran snapped. "We'll take you back to the village!"

"Okay." Jim shrugged.

Hans stepped toward him, and Ponga Jim started to follow Albran. But suddenly his foot slipped in the blood and he plunged forward, his head smashing into Albran's back and knocking him through the door into a sprawled heap on the path outside. Tumbling across him, Jim rolled over, scrambled to his feet and dove into the night and the jungle.

Thomsen snapped a quick shot into the night, and Ponga Jim grinned as it went yards from its object. After his first plunging run had carried him through the thick wall of jungle, Jim had stopped dead still. To move meant to make noise. He realized suddenly that he was clutching a bit of paper from the desk, picked up at the moment Albran discovered him. He thrust it in his pocket.

Back at the bungalow, Albran was shouting orders at Thomsen and Hans. Nearby, Doc Fife was talking in low tones with the man who had come up with him, a man whose face Ponga Jim could not distinguish.

Gradually Jim worked around a thick clump of ferns. Slowly, carefully, he worked his way back from the clearing. For a half hour he tried nothing but the most careful movement. Then he struck out, moving more boldly, and found the bank of a small stream. He stepped in carefully, found it shallow, and began to wade downstream toward the shore.

Walking in the water made travel faster, and Jim had time to think. He didn't know why Bent Frazer had written him after all this time. He had no idea what Kim Rinehart would be doing there or why he should be killed or, if his theory was right, and Kim had been killed by mistake, just why anyone should want to kill Frazer.

And where did Albran fit in? The Dutch resident was a recent appointee, although he had been in the islands for some time, despite frequent trips back to the Netherlands. Yet, somehow, Jim couldn't believe that he didn't know more than he had any right to know. How had he happened on the scene so soon? And where had Doc Fife come from? Who was the man with him? And who was the man who had passed Jim in the darkness?

He was glad when he got back to the shore and could use his flashlight to signal the nightwatch on the *Semiramis*. Yet when he turned in he was no closer to a solution. . . .

Ponga Jim awakened to a banging on his door. Then he heard Slug Brophy, his chief mate, roar:

"Skipper! Wake up, will you? A couple of Dutch coppers out

here want to put the pinch on you. Shall I drop the anchor on 'em?"

Jim sat up on his bunk. "Let them come aboard," he said finally. "I'll see them in the salon. And tell Li I want some breakfast."

Karl Albran, his lean face dark and ugly, was waiting in the salon when Ponga Jim came out. With him was Doc Fife and another man whom Jim recognized instantly without giving any indication of it. A fourth man came in a moment later, and Jim's eyes narrowed slightly before he smiled. Essen, he thought.

He sat down. "Don't mind if I eat, do you? Nothing like a few ham and eggs to set a man up."

"I suppose you know," Albran said icily, "what you can get for resisting an officer?"

Jim chuckled. "Sure, but I also know what I could get walking down a trail ahead of a man who wanted me dead, too. And I don't want any."

"Are you insinuating that I—"

Jim nodded. "You're darned right I am." He took a mouthful of ham and eggs. "I'm not playing poker this time, Albran," he said. "That walk down the mountain last night in the wet didn't suit me a little bit. I don't know what this racket is all about, but your part of it smells."

"Why, you—" Albran's face turned crimson with anger. "I'll—"

"No, you won't," Jim said quietly. "If you tried it I'd slap your jaws off. And even if you wanted to use the law, you can't use it on my ship. I've got a crew here, mister, a tough crew. So don't get any fancy ideas."

"I think," Fife said, interrupting, "that Mr. Bonner and I"—(so Colonel Sutherland of the British Intelligence was now Mr. Bonner, Jim thought)—"have convinced Mr. Albran that it is highly improbable that you would kill a man who had been your friend, and without reason. However, there must be an investigation, and Mr. Bonner here, who has had some business connections with Benton Frazer, is anxious the case be cleared up. We thought you might help us."

Jim shrugged and then told them of receiving a message

from Frazer and of what followed. He told it casually, carelessly, eating all the while.

"How about the message?" Bonner asked. "Did that give you any information?"

Jim reached into his coat pocket and tossed it on the table. It read:

COME AT ONCE. SOMETHING RIGHT DOWN
YOUR ALLEY. TELL NO ONE. IMPORTANT YOU
ARRIVE BEFORE THE FIFTH.
                                        FRAZER.

"You have no idea what he wanted?" Fife asked. "Had he said anything previously that would be a clue?"

"Listen," Jim said. "I hadn't seen Frazer or heard from him in ten years. We worked some together but we were never what you'd call friends."

"I'm sorry about last night," Albran said suddenly. "If I'd thought, I'd have realized the truth. A few days ago Frazer discharged a Papuan, a former headhunter. Obviously, he killed him for revenge and then fled to New Guinea with the head."

Ponga Jim chuckled. "No soap, pal."

"What do you mean?" Essen said. "Is it not obvious if the head is gone that a headhunter must take it? Who else had use for heads?"

Jim chuckled. "Whoever killed Kim didn't know I was going to come along so conveniently and be accused. He wanted Frazer out of the way, because Frazer knew something. But he didn't want any investigation or questions asked. So he took the head, thinking it would be passed off as a headhunter's job."

"Why couldn't it be?" Bonner asked.

"Simply because," Jim said drily, "headhunters do everything according to habit and custom. The removal of a victim's head follows a set pattern. Papuans always do it in the same manner, and rather neatly. Our friend who knocked off Kim just hacked off the head, not knowing his Papuan customs. As I

101

said," Jim looked up, grinning at Essen, "the guy who figured
that one out was a dumb cluck with a head like a cabbage."

"Then you believe Frazer, or rather, Rinehart, was killed by
a white man?" Fife asked thoughtfully.

Ponga Jim nodded. "I sure do. Furthermore," he added,
"Frazer is still around somewhere, still ready to tell what he
knows. Find him and you'll blow the lid off more than Kim
Rinehart's murder. And when you begin to get suspects, ask
them one question."

"What?" Albran demanded.

"Ask them: 'What do you know about the Well of the Unholy
Light?'!"

Silence gripped the salon, and Jim saw Fife watching Essen.
The man's face was set and stiff. He was staring at Ponga Jim,
his glance fairly ablaze with hatred.

"What do you mean?" Bonner asked. "What is the Well of
the Unholy Light?"

"Back up on the slope of Gam Konora is a well that shows a
peculiar, misty glow at night," Jim explained. "It is phosphorescent or something. You can't trace the origin of the light,
either. There's a *batu paduran* there. In other words, a stone
city. It isn't so very far from here. A day's travel if you know
the trails."

"What does it have to do with this murder?" Fife asked.

Ponga Jim Mayo got up slowly, reaching for his cap.

"That's your problem," he said seriously. "But whoever killed
Rinehart will answer to me. He wasn't my friend, but we
fought a couple of wars together, and men who do that don't
fail each other. Above all, he was killed for something he
wanted to tell me. So," Jim looked first at Essen and then at
Albran, "I'm declaring myself in for the duration!"

After they had gone, Jim stood staring out the porthole
thoughtfully. The rain had begun again, a cold, slanting rain.
He looked toward the green shores of Halmahera, looming
gray now. He had a sense of impending danger that left him

restless and ill at ease. Unconsciously, his hand strayed to the butt of his heavy Colt.

Frazer had stumbled on something big, he knew. But what? The only clue he had that wasn't available to them all from the beginning was the slip of paper from the desk in Frazer's cabin. It had been torn, and just enough remained to tell him the words had been "Well of the Unholy Light." And Jim knew about the well, somewhere up on the slopes of Gam Konora, over five thousand feet of active volcano and a taboo region, rarely visited by anyone, native or white.

That Colonel Sutherland, masquerading as Bonner, was around, offered ample evidence that this was something international in scope. It also meant that somewhere in the vicinity Major William Arnold would be working on the problem.

Ponga Jim grinned. He and William were to brush elbows again. But where, he wondered then, did Kim Rinehart fit into the picture? How did he happen to be on the spot when the killer arrived for Frazer?

Yet whatever was in the wind was too big for Essen. The man was dangerous, but not the type to lead any action as big as this must be. Albran was Dutch but, like a scattering of his countrymen, was obviously pro-Nazi. Fife and Sutherland, he had learned, had been hunting near Mount Sabu and so had an alibi for being on hand. But what was the answer?

There seemed only one chance of finding out—to go to the Well of the Unholy Light.

The rain had ceased and the clouds were breaking up when Ponga Jim Mayo rounded the shoulder of Gam Konora and looked down on the steep canyon that separated him from the plateau where the well was supposed to be. He hesitated, staring down.

The canyon was a fearful gash in the earth and washed by a charging, plunging mountain stream. Across from him the wall of the mountain broke, and he could look past it to the plateau beyond. A huge stone column reared from the jungle, at least a hundred feet high, and beyond it was a square tower, half fallen to ruins. But between them, between the plateau and Mayo, was the gash in the earth.

It was then he saw the bridge, not more than a hundred feet away, but blending its color so easily with the rock as to be almost invisible, a swaying bridge of hemp rope, native-made, suspended across the three hundred feet of the canyon. Below it was the stream. Jim looked down and then started for the swaying bridge.

It trembled giddily at his first step, but he did not hesitate. Yet he had taken no more than three steps before he had a feeling that he was being watched. Carefully, yet with seeming carelessness, his eyes searched the jumble of rocks he was approaching. There was nothing, no movement or indication of life.

He walked on quietly, but managing to weave just a little on the swaying bridge, enough to make the chances of hitting him with the first shot a little more difficult. But he had reached the end of the bridge and had his feet on the rock before anything happened. Then a cool, deep voice spoke suddenly from the rocks:

"You stand still now and answer me some questions."

Ponga Jim stopped. "Okay, pal. Let's have them."

"What's your handle, mister? What name you go by?"

"The name is Mayo," Jim said pleasantly. "They call me Ponga Jim."

"Where you get that 'Ponga' part?"

"From the village of Ponga-Ponga in French Equatorial Africa. Anything else?"

"If you was looking for a man you knew in Manchuria, and he was in Fez, where would you look? And if he was in Algiers?"

Jim's eyes narrowed. "In Fez, I'd look in the long room behind a leatherworker's stall in the street near the Green Mosque. In Algiers, I would go to the place of Mahr-el-din in the Kasbah."

A powerfully built black man came from behind a cluster of

boulders and stepped down with his big hand outthrust. He wore a dark red shirt and a pair of blue dungarees. Two big guns were strapped to his hips, and a high-powered rifle was in the hollow of his arm. Two bandoliers of cartridges crossed his chest.

"How you, Captain Mayo?" he said cheerfully. "I'm Big London. A friend to Bent Frazer. He told me if anything happened to him I was to get down here and watch out for you, that you'd be along, and that you'd answer those questions. That way, I'd know you. But I'd have known you, anyway."

Jim shook hands, sizing up the mighty black man with appreciation.

"What's up?" he asked. "Where's Frazer?"

"They got him down there by the well. They got a couple of hundred men down there."

"How many?" Jim was incredulous. "Did you say two hundred?"

Big London nodded. "That's right. They've been bringing them in planes. Dropped twenty here last night from parachutes. But Frazer, he said to start nothing until you got here." Then he added, "Those men are Japanese, all but two or three."

Led swiftly by the big black man, Ponga Jim slipped through the rocks until they could get a good view of the city. It was scarcely that, just a temple. Now it was all in ruins, and a small circle of stone houses was surrounded by a fallen wall. The stone plaza had been cleared of debris, but was not large enough for a plane to land. But even as they watched they saw several men carrying rifles from one of the buildings. A cool voice behind them spoke:

"How do you do, Captain?"

Jim wheeled. Five men in a neat rank stood behind them. Four were Japanese soldiers, their rifles ready. The fifth was Heittn, a Nazi agent.

"See how easily a man is captured when he grows confident?" Heittn said, speaking over his shoulder to the soldiers. Then, to Jim, "We knew Frazer had communicated with you, so we were ready this time." Heittn's narrow, heavy-lidded eyes shifted to the black man. "We won't need you," he said and lifted his automatic. Without a second's hesitation, he fired.

Big London had started to leap, but his body turned slowly and plunged down the steep slope of shale. For sixty feet his body slid and then brought up against a boulder.

Ponga Jim's eyes went hard.

"That was a dirty stunt!" he said.

"Of course." Heittn shrugged. "Why not? We want you to use for bait. He would have been excess baggage."

It was an hour before they finished questioning him. Heittn had begun it when they got him safely below and in a stone room. Four bulky Germans, an Italian, and three Japanese had entered with him. The door was closed. His hands had been bound. Then Heittn had walked up and struck him in the mouth. Then he stepped back and kicked Jim across the shins.

Ponga Jim moved like lightning, kicking out himself. The kick caught Heittn in the pit of the stomach and rolled him across the room. Instantly, the five men hit Jim at once. He was knocked to his knees, jerked to his feet, and driven into the wall and battered. Then Heittn pushed his way through the crowd, his face a mask of fury.

"So?" he snarled. "You will, will you?"

He had a short length of rubber hose, and he slammed Jim wickedly across the shoulders with it. Then came a powerful blow over the head that drove Jim to his knees. Heittn hit him twice more before he could get up.

Ponga Jim was desperate. He knew what such a beating could do to a man. He had seen the Gestapo work before. But he lunged to his feet, determined to go down without a whimper, without whining. Heittn battered him, then the others. The Italian named Calzo took his turn at the hose.

"What's the matter?" Jim said drily. "Can't you hit a man unless he's tied?"

Calzo's face flamed with anger, and he dealt Mayo a terrific blow over the head that knocked him into oblivion.

When Jim opened his eyes he was conscious of pain. His body was afire with agony. He lay very still, staring up into darkness. Then he tried to move, but was bound hand and foot. His stirrings brought a voice from the abysmal darkness.

"Jim?" It was Frazer. "Are you all right?"

Jim groaned. "All right, nothing! I'm beaten half blind. Those rats used a hose on me."

"You're not the only one. What happened to London?"

"Heittn shot him. You alone here?"

"No!" It was a new voice. "They got me, too. Right after you stumbled onto Rinehart's body."

Jim was startled. "William?" he gasped. "Can't you keep out of trouble? What's the gag, anyway?"

Frazer said, "Remember the *Copenhagen?* The German freighter that went Danish in a hurry when the war broke out? She's down here with a cargo of eighteen-foot baby submarines. They are built to submerge to five hundred feet, and each one carries a torpedo. They plan on sewing a string of them clear across the Indies, with the *Copenhagen* as mother ship. She can carry about fifty of them without much trouble. Todahe Bay is the main base."

"It's a good spot," Major Arnold said. "An almost closed harbor, unseen until you're almost inside."

"Todahe Bay?" Jim said thoughtfully. "That's close by." He lay quiet a minute. "What are they doing here?"

"It's a torpedo plant," Frazer said. "They have natural heat here when they need it, they have power from that stream down below, and because of the well, no native will come near. The well is a big pool in the rock, opening to an underground lake, and the water is made phosphorescent by some growth in it. Like seawater."

"But how do they get the torpedoes down to the subs?" Jim asked.

Frazer shrugged. "I don't know. Rinehart tipped me off to all this. He was a German, you know. They rang him in on the deal, and he was smart enough to play along and keep his mouth shut. Then he came to me with the story. Somebody killed Rinehart by mistake. I picked that up from one of the guards this morning."

Jim lay very quiet. He knew now that something had to be done. Fifty pocket submarines could create havoc in the East Indies. With luck they might cut shipping in half in a matter of weeks.

There was a sound of feet. Then the door rattled and swung back on its hinges. Jim noticed then that the room was carved from solid rock. He was jerked to his feet and found himself facing Karl Albran, Essen, and the guard.

"So!" Albran sneered. "You are so smart, eh? You walk right into a trap. I knew it would happen!"

"Untie his feet," Essen told the guard. "Heittn would see you now. We are using you for bait. Bait to end the existence of the *Semiramis!*"

As the guard untied his feet, it was now or never, Jim thought. He felt the rope fall loose about his ankles and waited until the guard had drawn it clear. Then he kicked, short and hard.

The toe of his shoe caught the kneeling guard in the solar plexus. Then Jim lunged, smashing Essen full in the chest with his head, knocking him into the wall. Instantly Karl Albran sprang into the dark cell, his gun up. But, momentarily blinded by the darkness, he stood stock-still staring. In that second, Arnold jerked his bound body to a sitting position and butted the Dutchman behind the knees. The man staggered, and before he could regain his balance, Arnold rolled against his ankles. The man hit the floor hard, and Frazer fell across him.

Ponga Jim jerked the guard to his feet with the one hand he had managed to jerk free. Jim pushed him away and then hit him with the free hand. And as he fell, he grabbed the man's knife and cut himself loose just as Essen made a dive for the door. He leaped after him, but Albran had struggled free of the bound men and was on his feet. He swung a wild blow that hit

Jim on the ear, and then charged in, punching wildly. At the same instant, Essen wheeled and tackled him from behind.

Then, suddenly, Big London dropped from somewhere above the door. Stepping into the room he grabbed Essen and smashed the Nazi into unconsciousness. Jim butted Albran and then hit him in the stomach. The Dutchman went down, and Jim wheeled to cut Arnold free as the black man freed Frazer.

"I thought you were dead," Jim managed to gasp.

"He shot as I fell, missed me, so I kept on falling," the black man explained. Then Big London sprang for the door, turned, and caught a ledge over the cell door, pulling himself up. Lost in the shadows above the cell door was a black tunnel. He pulled himself in, extended a hand to Frazer, and then to Arnold.

Jim glanced back into the cell; then he pulled himself up and followed Big London at a rapid trot down the floor of the tunnel. In a few minutes they came to another tunnel and crawling out, were in the clear.

Silently, Big London dug into a bunch of ferns and passed out guns.

"I stole them," he boasted. "Right from under their eyes."

"What now?" Frazer demanded. "Where do we go from here?"

"Back," Jim said grimly. "We're going back down there and blast thunder out of things."

"But there's two hundred of them!" Frazer protested.

"Sure," Ponga Jim agreed. "One of you is going to the *Semiramis* for men. Or rather, you're going back across the bridge and signal from the shoulder of the mountain. They'll be watching. I told them to."

Grabbing a rifle, Ponga Jim ran to a cluster of boulders overlooking the stone plaza below. Japanese soldiers were spilling from all the buildings, rifles in hand. Instantly, he threw his gun to his shoulder and fired. One of the soldiers stopped in midstride and plunged over on his face. Beside the Yank,

Frazer, Arnold, and Big London were pouring a devastating fire into the square. But suddenly a machine gun broke loose from the tower, and they were forced back.

"You're it, London!" Jim said. "Beat it for the shoulder of the mountain. When you can see the *Semiramis*, flash the mirror you'll find there by the lightning-struck tree. Get it?"

The black man wheeled and was gone like a flash.

"Come on," Jim said grimly. "We're going back down the tunnel!"

"What?" Frazer demanded. "Are you crazy?"

"In a minute," Jim said, "this mountain here will be flooded with Japanese and Nazis. The bridge will be covered, and we won't have a chance. So we're going back down there where they would never expect us to be!"

It was a silent group of men that crept back along the tunnel. When they looked down into the passage outside their cell, it was empty. One by one they dropped down. Then, gun in hand, Jim led the way down the passage.

This passage must come out in one of the stone buildings, he thought, and must be close to the well. And that well was something he must see. Somehow the *Copenhagen* and her cargo of submarines must be stopped. Somehow this plant must be wrecked. The problem, he knew, was to find how they got torpedoes to the ships on Todahe Bay. It was almost two thousand feet from the plateau where they now were to the surface of the bay. And several miles over rough, mountainous trail. No sort of country to be transporting torpedoes in. There had to be another way, and Ponga Jim had a hunch.

They emerged from the passage in a square stone building near the tower. Outside the door the square seemed empty, yet they knew there were men in the tower above and probably others around close. Eyes narrowed, Jim studied the square thoughtfully. The tracks of some sort of a cart or truck led from the tower toward a cluster of rocks under the overhang of the cliff. The tracks had cut through the layer of soil to the solid rock of the plateau. Whatever they had carried had been heavy.

"What next, Jim?" asked Arnold softly.

"Look!" Jim indicated the marks of the wheels. "They've wheeled their torpedoes in that direction. Well, that's the way we're going! From now on it's going to be a running fight until we reach the shelter of those rocks. Beyond that, I don't know what we'll find. But I've got fifty that says it's the Well of the Unholy Light!"

"Let's go!" Frazer said. "These monkeys asked for it. Let 'em take it!"

Gun in hand, Jim sprang through the door. A Japanese sentry was standing across the plaza. And before he could get his gun up, Jim shot him in the stomach. Then they started on a dead run for the rocks, just a hundred yards away. Abruptly then, a myriad of tiny spurts of dust jumped all around them. Jim heard a curse and knew someone was hit. He wheeled, fired, and then ran on. He was almost to the rocks when suddenly Essen sprang from behind them, holding a submachine gun. His eyes glinting with triumph, he jerked the gun to his shoulder.

Ponga Jim stopped dead still and lifted his own gun. The automatic bucked in his hand, then again. Essen backed up, astonished. Then slowly he pitched over on his face and lay still. But already Ponga Jim was beyond him, with Major Arnold at his side. It was only then that they saw Frazer. Bent was down on his knees, facing the opposite direction, his whole side stained with blood. He was firing slowly, methodically. Even as they saw him, Frazer's Luger spoke, and a Japanese on the tower toppled forward, dead. Then a burst of machine gun bullets from the tower hit Bent Frazer, fairly lifting him from the ground.

Ponga Jim Mayo turned, his face hard, staring around him. They stood on a narrow ledge of rock around the well. The water did glow with a peculiar light, visible in the shadows of the pool under the overhanging cliff. But there was nothing, only the well, a pool probably fifty feet across.

"Well," Arnold said. "Here we are. Now what?"

"Keep your shirt on, William," said Ponga Jim grimly. "Maybe I've guessed wrong, but I don't think so."

"This is a fine time to be in doubt!" Arnold snapped. "I think—"

Suddenly the waters of the pool began to stir, as with the heavings of some subterranean monster. Then a conning tower broke the surface, and after it—the deck of a submarine!

"William," said Jim, "watch outside. I'm taking this ship!" He turned quickly. "Don't let them see your face until they are out of there," he whispered hoarsely, "and for the love of Mike, don't shoot!"

Breathless, they heard the conning tower hatch open and the sound of feet on the rounded surface of the sub. Then they heard a second pair of feet. A guttural voice spoke harshly in German, and Ponga Jim turned.

The two men, one a Nazi, the other the Italian, Calzo, were standing on the sub, just about to step ashore. Arnold pulled the trigger of his gun, but it clicked on an empty chamber. Coolly, Ponga Jim shot the Nazi over the belt buckle twice. As the man fell forward, Jim pivoted and snapped a quick shot at Calzo, who was hurriedly aiming his gun. The bullet struck the Italian's gun, knocking it from his hand.

But Calzo was game. With a snarl of fury, he leaped ashore. Out of the corner of his eye Jim saw Arnold feverishly reloading his automatic and heard a wild yell from the plaza. Then Calzo sprang at him, swinging a powerful right. Jim ducked under the blow and hooked low and hard for Calzo's ribs. The punch smashed home with driving force. Then Jim stepped in with a sweeping right uppercut that knocked the Italian off the edge and into the well. He sank like a stone. Now Arnold was firing desperately.

"Quick, Jim!" he yelled. "Here they come! At least fifty of them!"

"We've got a sub. Come on!" Jim snapped.

*   *   *

Arnold snapped one quick shot out of the conning tower and then slammed the hatch shut. In a minute he had swung into the engineer's compartment, and with Jim at the periscope they submerged slowly.

"You got any idea what this is all about?" Arnold snapped. "This isn't just a toy, you know."

"We're submerging," Jim said cheerfully. "We're going down around five hundred feet. Then we'll find a passage and get out of it into Todahe Bay. There we'll find the *Copenhagen* loaded with submarines, and we'll shoot her one in the pants—I hope."

"*You* hope!" Arnold said sarcastically. "You mean, *I* hope! And if something happens and you're wrong?"

"We wash out," Jim said simply and shrugged.

"Yeah?" William said. "That's okay for you, but I've got a date with a girl in Makassar."

Slowly the sub sank deeper and deeper. Ponga Jim wiped the sweat from his brow. After all, maybe it wouldn't work. Still, the sub had just come up. It had to come from somewhere.

"You mean Kitty, that dancer from Manila?" Jim asked, grinning.

Arnold was astonished. "How did you know?"

Jim chuckled. "She tells me about all the strange people she meets," he said. "Interesting girl, Kitty."

The sub was still sinking, and for a moment they were still.

"Pal," Arnold said suddenly, "are you sure these things will take five hundred? That's awful deep! About two hundred deeper than a regular sub should take."

Jim stared at the depth gauge as the needle flickered past 200. 250—300—350—

"Maybe we've missed the outlet," Arnold said.

"You would think of that," Jim growled.

The pressure was building up at a terrific rate. He tried to see something, but the water around was black and still.

Four hundred!

"If it's anywhere, it'll be pretty quick now, William," Jim said. "If it isn't, we're dead pigeons."

Four hundred and fifty!

"Do you suppose your crew got to that bunch upstairs?" Major Arnold asked.

"I'd bet my life on that. That bunch of fighting fools never misses."

Five hundred!

Nothing but blackness and the close, heavy heat of the sub. Then he saw it suddenly—the outline of an opening illuminated by the powerful light of the sub. Slowly, carefully, he eased the sub into the blackness.

"Like floating down a sewer," Jim said aloud.

"I wouldn't know," Arnold said. "I never floated down any sewers."

Suddenly they were out, and then they were rising.

"This bay isn't deep," Arnold said, "so we haven't far to come up. When we went down we were up in the mountains. So stand by that torpedo."

"Thar she blows!" Ponga Jim said suddenly. "About two points on the bow. Stand by while I run this crate in a little bit. I'm going to give her both barrels. I thought these babies only carried one torpedo, but they have two!"

And with that he released both torpedoes.

All was quiet, then—

The shuddering impact of the explosion made them gasp for breath. Then, a split second later, the second!

"Two strikes, William!" shouted Ponga Jim. "Come on, we're heading for the Ibu River and the *Semiramis* at top speed. We hit the *Copenhagen* one forward and one aft. She won't float ten minutes!"

Ponga Jim ran shaky fingers through his hair. Suddenly he realized that he was sitting in trousers soggy with blood.

"William," he said, "those Nazis clipped me. I'm shot."

"Where?" Arnold yelled.

Jim looked down. "Nuts! I was just sitting in a paint bucket!"

There was silence for a moment, and then Arnold spoke up:

"Honest, Jim. Have you been out with Kitty? What's she like?"

"She's wonderful!" Ponga Jim said, grinning. "Why, Kitty is—" Red fluid cascaded over him. "Hey!" he roared, blinking. "What did you throw at me?"

"The rest of the paint bucket," Arnold said grimly.

AUTHOR'S NOTE

WEST FROM SINGAPORE

Most of the stories in this collection were written before the Japanese attack on Pearl Harbor. The Netherlands East Indies, as they were then called, were a valuable prize. Japan's move into that area had not begun when the first stories were written, but it began soon after, and only a few small warships were available to protect the islands. Aside from a wide variety of other useful products, the Indonesian islands offered an easy supply of oil, as well as tin, most of which came from Malaysia, just to the north. My first trip into the region was as a seaman on a freighter carrying pipe and drilling equipment to Balikpapan, in Borneo.

These were the islands Columbus was trying to reach when he sailed west from Spain. Contrary to popular tradition, he did not have to convince anybody that the world was round. All those to whom he talked already knew that. The reason he was refused help was that his estimates of the distance he had to sail were based on the mistaken figures of Ptolemy, which made the world much smaller. In Portugal, for example, the people he approached were perfectly aware he could not reach the Indies in the time projected.

WEST FROM SINGAPORE

A crisp voice at Ponga Jim's elbow said: "Captain Mayo?"
Ponga Jim turned. His white-topped cap with its captain's
insignia was pushed back on his dark, curly hair, and his broad,
powerful shoulders stretched the faded khaki coat.

Colonel Roland Warren could see the bulge of the .45 automatic in its shoulder holster, and there was disapproval in his
eyes. From the woven-leather sandals to the carelessly worn
cap, Ponga Jim Mayo was anything but what he believed a
ship's captain should be.

"I'm Mayo," Jim held out his hand, "and you'll be Colonel
Warren? Nice to have you aboard."

Warren nodded. "My men will be along directly. May I see
their quarters now? Will their cabins be amidships?"

"Sorry, Colonel, but they'll have to bunk in the 'tween
decks. We don't carry passengers as a rule and only have three
cabins available. Two of them are occupied. I'd planned to put
you and Captain Aldridge in the other."

"The 'tween decks?" Warren was incredulous. "My men are
officers, I'll have you know, and—"

"Sorry," Jim repeated. "Officers, men, or gods, they ride the
'tween decks or swim. You'll have to remember, Colonel," he
added drily, "that this is wartime. People don't get what they
want. They take what they get."

"Very well." Warren's blue eyes were frosty. "However, you

119

had no business taking passengers aboard for such a trip. The Admiralty won't approve. I suppose you know that?"

"Colonel Warren," Jim said quietly, "for all I care the Admiralty can go to blazes. My first duty is to these passengers."

The flyers were coming aboard, a pink-cheeked, healthy lot, all except two in their late teens or early twenties. These two turned toward the bridge. Ponga Jim's eyes sharpened.

The men were both as tall as Ponga Jim himself, and one of them was as heavy. He was a powerfully built man with rusty-red hair, freckles, and a scar along his jawbone. His nose was broken and slightly askew. His manner was cocky, aggressive.

He stepped up to Mayo with his hand out. "Hi, Jim!" he said, grinning. "Long time no see."

Mayo's eyes brightened.

"Ring Wallace! I haven't seen you since China!"

The second man watched them with interest. He was wiry, handsome in a dark, saturnine way, and there was something crisp and efficient in his manner.

"Captain Henry Aldridge," Warren said, "my second in command."

Aldridge bowed from the hips, smiling.

"How are you, Captain? I've been hearing some interesting things about you. That Qasavara affair, for instance."

"Yeah," Ponga Jim looked at him with interest. "It was an ugly business. But I never look for trouble, I just take care of what comes over my way."

"I hope," Warren said drily, "that you won't find it necessary to indulge in any of your freebooting expeditions on this trip. I can't say that we Britishers approve of pirates!"

"No?" Jim said quizzically. "Ever hear of Sir Francis Drake?"

Warren started as if struck, and his eyes blazed. Then his face flushed, and he spun on his heel and went below. Ring Wallace grinned and winked at Jim.

"He's all right. Just needs a little seasoning. He's a good man, Jim."

120

Aldridge studied them both carefully. "I think Wallace is right," he said then. "Colonel Warren *is* a good man. But I think we Englishmen and Australians have a little to say about freebooting, eh, Mayo?"

Jim looked at him curiously. "Which are you? You don't have the lingo, somehow."

"Australian," Aldridge said. "From back in the bush, but educated on the Continent."

Slug Brophy and Gunner Millan came up to the deck. Jim turned to them.

"All set, Skipper. Number five battened down, all standing by fore and aft," reported Slug.

"Then send Selim up to the wheel and let's get out of here."

He watched his mates go, one forward, one aft. Selim, his dark, pockmarked, knife-scarred face cool and expressionless, came to the wheel.

"You've an odd crew," Aldridge said. "Quite a mixture."

Jim nodded. "Selim and Sakim are brothers. A strange contradiction themselves. Afridis from the Afghan hills who went to sea. Used to be smugglers on the Red Sea and down the coast of Africa. Big London is from the Congo. Lyssy is a Toradjas from the Celebes. Tupa and Longboy are Bugis. Boma is a Dyak. They are a mixture. And all fighting men."

"The Gunner there," he nodded aft, "did ten years in His Majesty's Navy. Brophy was in the American Marines, went to sea, and then was with me in the Chaco and in China."

"What about your passengers, Captain?" Aldridge asked politely. "I haven't seen them around."

"You won't," Ponga Jim replied shortly. He stood by with a megaphone, directing the movements of the ship. When the tug was cast off, he took her out himself, watching the endless panorama of Singapore harbor, the hundreds of ships of all sizes and kinds, the white houses, red islands, and dark green foliage.

Sakim came up the ladder with a yellow envelope. "A message, Nakhoda," he said, bowing.

Jim ripped it open. It was terse, to the point.

121

PROCEED WITH CAUTION. BELIEVE RAIDER
INFORMED OF EVERY ACTION. ARMED MER-
CHANTMAN OF TEN THOUSAND TONS OPER-
ATING IN INDIAN OCEAN. YOU MAY HAVE
ENEMY AGENT ABOARD. ORDERS HAVE GONE
OUT YOU ARE NOT TO REACH THE RED SEA.
LUCK.

ARNOLD.

Jim passed the message to Brophy and Millan. "William's on
the job," he said. "Looks like our work's cut out for us."

Millan looked aft thoughtfully. "I don't like that Warren," he
said. "Could it be him?"

"Might be anybody," Jim replied. "Not necessarily a German. A lot of people who don't see beyond the surface think
dictatorships are best. They forget their supposed efficiency is
because they censor news of mistakes, or shoot them. Warren
is Australian, but he might be that kind of person. On the
other hand, there's Wallace."

"You and him have always been on opposite sides," Slug
suggested, "maybe—"

"We've got to keep a weather eye on them all," Jim said.
"But the main job will be getting to the Red Sea. At least one
raider has us marked for sinking, and we've got thirty planes
aboard and twenty-three flyers, to say nothing of two passengers and some munitions." Jim's jaw set hard and his eyes
narrowed. "And we're going through if we have to sink a
couple of pocket battleships!"

Day in and day out the *Semiramis* steamed south by east,
through Banko Strait, around Sumatra, and through the Straits
of Sunda and into the wide waters of the Indian Ocean. On
deck and on the bridge there was an endless watch.

On the after deck, the two 5.9s painted to resemble booms
and further disguised with blocks hooked to their muzzles,

were never without a crew. The gun crews slept on deck in the shadow of their guns, ready and waiting.

Still the *Semiramis* headed south and a little west. The shipping lanes for India and the Red Sea fell behind. The lanes for the Cape were further south. When they reached the tenth parallel, Ponga Jim changed the course to due west.

Twice, Ring Wallace came to the bridge. His face was grave and his eyes hard. He said nothing. Each time he looked pointedly at the sun, indicating to Mayo that he knew they were off the course for Aden, but Jim ignored him.

It was the day he changed course to due west that Colonel Warren came to the bridge. His eyes were cold and suspicious.

"I want to know what you're doing this far south," he demanded.

Mayo started to speak sharply and then shrugged. "Come here," he said patiently. He stepped into the chart room. "Look," he pointed to the chart. "We're off our course, but we're on a better one. How much shipping have you seen in the last couple of days?"

"Why, none," Warren said, puzzled. "What has that to do with it?"

"Simply that if there's a raider active, he'll stay close to the shipping lanes. Looking for us down here would be like looking for one particular fly in Dakar. But when we turn north—"

"But we're south of any possible help," Warren protested. "And what about the radio? Sparks tells me you've ordered no messages to leave the ship, no reports, nothing."

"Right. Radio makes a trail. My orders are to get this ship to my destination on the Red Sea. I'm going without convoy. This is my ship, and I'm going through."

Warren hesitated and then went below, but he was not satisfied. Ponga Jim rubbed his chin and looked after him thoughtfully.

The tension mounted daily. Everyone watched the horizon now, when they weren't watching the blank, unspeaking doors of the two cabins. But the passengers remained unseen. The steward went to them with one guard, and neither man would talk.

Ring Wallace, pointedly wearing a gun, had taken to idling about the deck amidships. The R.A.F. men were uneasy. Only the crew of the *Semiramis* seemed undisturbed.

One night Ponga Jim got up, slipped on his coat, and casually checked the load in his automatic. It was habitual action, born of struggle and the need for a gun that was ready. Then he picked up his cap and stepped toward the door.

"Hold it."

Mayo froze. That would be Wallace. He turned slowly to face him. Ring was just inside the opposite door, his face grim. The gun in his hand was steady.

"Why the artillery?" Jim asked mildly.

"Mayo," Ring said slowly, "I've known you for about ten years. We ain't seen things eye to eye, but a good part of the time you have been nearer right than me. This time, I ain't so sure."

"You asking for a showdown, Ring?"

"Sure, I want to know what we're doing hundreds of miles off our course. I want to know who your passengers are. I want to know what your intentions are.

"Maybe for the first time in my life I'm doing something without thinking of money. I'm going to the Near East to fight because I don't like dictatorships."

Wallace broke off to give Mayo a hard, direct glance and then plunged on in a flat-toned voice.

"Sure, I know a lot of this stuff is the old blarney. It's propaganda. England's leadership has been coming apart at the seams for years. Her people are all right, but at the top they've been a lot of wealthy and titled highbinders. They don't want a democratic England. It's the same way in the States. When you look for pro-Nazis look in the higher brackets of income, not the lower.

"But their time is past. The real England's coming to the top in this war. I figure democracy with all its faults has an edge over anything else. England and America, battling side by side, will prove that to Germany and Japan. Well, I've fought for money, and I've fought for the heck of it. This time it's for an idea.

"So maybe I ain't so smart. You could always outfigure me, Jim Mayo, but this cargo gets through or you go over the side—feet first. I'm not kidding, either."

"Put up the heater, Ring. This time it looks like we're pitching for the same club. Look!" He took him to the chart. "Somewhere in this ocean we're scheduled to be sunk. There's the route for low-powered steamers. Here's the route we could have taken. It's dollars to guilders both routes are covered. So what do I do? I stop the radio and then drop out of sight. To all intents and purposes we're lost!

"Look here," Jim handed a message to Wallace. "Sparks picked this up last night."

S.S. *RHYOLITE* SUNK WITH ALL HANDS TWO DAYS OUT OF SINGAPORE. S.S. *SEMIRAMIS* RE-PORTED MISSING. NO WORD SINCE LEAVING SUNDA.

"See? The Admiralty's worried. Intelligence is worried. But we're safe, and a third of the distance gone. Tonight, however, we change course. After that, anything can happen."

"So I'm a sucker," Ring said, grinning. "Chalk it up as a well-meant mistake. Be seeing you."

Hours passed slowly on the bridge. The night was dark and still. The air was heavy with heat. Along the horizon a bank of black clouds was building up, shot through from time to time with lightning. The barometer was falling, and Ponga Jim mopped his brow.

A sudden flash of lightning lit up a cloud like an incandescent globe. Mayo dropped his hands to the railing and stared.

By the brief glimpse he had seen something else. There, not

125

even a mile away was the black outline of a ship! Instantly, Jim stepped into the wheelhouse.

"Put her over easy," he said quietly. "Put her over three points and then hold it."

Instinctively, he knew the long, black ship was the raider. But with any luck he was going to slip away. Obviously, the raider's lookout hadn't seen him.

The *Semiramis* swung until her stern was almost toward the raider. Ponga Jim glanced aft as they started to pull away. Then almost before his eyes, and on his main deck, a light flashed. From over the way came the jangle of a bell.

Swiftly, he stepped to the speaking tube. "Red," he snapped. "This is it. Give her all you've got."

He sounded the signal for battle stations, and still in complete darkness, felt his ship coming to life. Millan emerged from his cabin and dashed aft. Other men appeared from out of nowhere.

Catching a gleam from aft, Jim knew the two 5.9s were swinging to cover the raider.

A gun from the German belched fire. The shell hit the sea off to port. Then a huge searchlight flashed on, and they were caught and pinned to the spot of light.

A signal flashed from the raider, and Sparks yelled, "He says stop or he'll sink us!"

"Tell him to try to sink us!" Jim roared. Grabbing the megaphone, he stepped into the wing of the bridge. "Let 'em have it, Gunner! Knock that light out of there!"

He took a quick glance around to locate the cloud. It was nearer now, a great, rolling, ominous mass shot through with vivid streaks. A shell crashed off to starboard, and then the 5.9s boomed, one-two.

A geyser of water leaped fifty feet to port of the advancing ship, and then the second shell exploded close off the starboard quarter.

"That rocked her!" Jim yelled. "Keep her weaving," he told the quartermaster.

"*Taiyib*," Sakim said quietly.

Despite the fact that the freighter was giving all she had, the raider was coming up fast. The guns were crashing steadily, but so far neither had scored a hit.

The black cloud was nearer now. Jim wheeled to the door of the pilothouse when there was a terrible concussion and he was knocked sprawling into the bulkhead.

Almost at once, he was on his feet, staggering, with blood running into his eyes from where his head had smashed into the doorjamb. The port wing of the bridge had been shot away.

Millan's guns crashed suddenly, shaking the deck, and both shots hit the raider.

The first pierced the bow just abaft the hawsepipe and exploded in the forepeak. The second smashed the gun on the foredeck into a heap of twisted metal.

"Hard aport!" Jim yelled. "Swing her!"

Then the storm burst around them with a roar, a sudden black squall that sent a blinding dash of rain over the ship.

A sea struck them and cascaded down over the deck, but the *Semiramis* straightened. Behind them a gun boomed. But struggling with a howling squall they had left all visibility behind them.

Slug Brophy came up the ladder. He was sweating and streaming with rain at the same time.

"Take her over," Jim directed briefly. "And drive her. Stay with this squall if you can."

Lyssy appeared on the deck below, his powerful brown body streaming with water.

"Go below and tell Colonel Warren I want all his men in the salon—*now!*" Jim bawled.

For a few minutes he stayed on the bridge, watching the storm. Then he went down to the salon. The flyers, their faces heavy with sleep, were gathered around the table. Only Warren and Aldridge appeared wide-awake. Aldridge was running a deck of cards through his long fingers, his dark, curious eyes on Mayo.

"What does this mean?" Warren asked. "Isn't it bad enough with a raider and a storm without getting us all up here?"

Ponga Jim ignored him. He looked around the table, his eyes glancing from one to the other.

"Before we left Sunda Strait," he began suddenly, "I had word there was an enemy agent aboard."

Warren stiffened. His eyes narrowed. Wallace let the legs of his chair down hard and leaned forward, elbows on his knees. Aldridge held the cards in his left hand and flicked the ash from his cigarette. His eyes shifted just a little, toward Wallace.

"Tonight," Jim went on, "I had concrete proof. We were slipping away in the darkness, unnoticed, when someone on the main deck flashed a light!"

"*What?*" Warren sat up straighter. "You've captured him?"

"No," Jim said. "I don't know for sure who he is. *But he's in this room!*"

Warren was on his feet, his face suffused with anger.

"I resent that!" he said sharply. "What about your own crew? These men are all mine. Why must one of them be the traitor? That's impudence! It's unfair!"

"It sounds like it," Mayo agreed, "but my crew have been with me a long time. Each of them has been in battle against Nazis. They have no love for them."

"Natives and renegades!" Warren protested angrily.

"But good men," Ponga Jim said quietly, his eyes dark and brilliant. "I've fought beside them. They aren't interested in ideologies. The traitor is."

He hesitated, looking around. "I wanted to warn you. One of you undoubtedly knows who the guilty man is. Just think. When you decide, no matter who it is, come to me.

"There are, as you know, raiders in this ocean looking for us. Our chances of reaching Aden without encountering one of them are small. Every hour that spy is aboard makes our risk greater. But whatever he does, he will have to be alone to do it. So stay together. *And under no circumstances must any man be found on deck alone!*"

"And the passengers?" Aldridge asked softly. "What of them? Those very mysterious passengers who never appear on deck. Mightn't one of them be the spy?"

"No," Jim said quietly. "There is no possibility of that."

He turned and left the salon, hurrying down the passage toward the two mysterious cabins. He tapped lightly on the door. There was a murmured word, and the door opened. Jim stepped inside, closing the cabin door softly.

Two people faced him, a man of perhaps fifty and a girl of twenty-five. The man was tall and finely built, with a dark, interested face and a military bearing. He got quickly to his feet, even as Jim's eyes met the girl's. General André Caillaux and his niece had been famous in the Paris that preceded the Nazi attack.

And for years in North Africa, General Caillaux had been one of the most loved and feared officers in the French army.

Known for daring and fair dealing as well, he had great influence among the men. So enormous was this influence that the wavering Pétain government sent him to a position in New Caledonia. Now, hoping that his prestige might swing the Foreign Legion and other powerful detachments to their side, the British were returning him to North Africa.

"How is it?" Caillaux asked quickly. "Is there trouble?"

"A brush with a raider." Jim's feet braced against the roll of the deck, and his knees bent slightly when it tipped. "We got away in a squall. Hit once, but no serious damage. We holed his bow enough to make trouble in this blow, and wrecked one of his guns."

"The Nazi agent?" Caillaux's voice was anxious.

Jim shrugged. "It's got me. Wallace has always been the sort to do anything for money. But this time I doubt it."

"Warren?"

"I don't know. He may be just officious, overly conscious of his new rank. And it might be a clever disguise."

"Who else could it be?" Jeanne asked. Her voice was husky.

"It might be anyone of the twenty-three. It might be Aldridge. He's a deep one. Never says much. But don't open the door for anyone but me."

He stepped out into the dark passageway and started to pull the door shut. He saw the flicker of the shadows a second too late, and then something smashed him alongside the head. He felt himself falling. But with a mighty effort, struggling against a black wave of unconsciousness, he held himself erect and swung blindly with his free hand. He missed. Something struck him again. But his hand clung to the door, and now he fell forward, pulling it shut.

As the lock clicked there was a snarl of impotent fury from his attacker. The man leaped at him, striking viciously at his head and face with a heavy blackjack. The attack was entirely soundless, for neither man had made a noise aside from that brief but angry snarl. Ponga Jim, groggy from the first blow, never had a chance. The pounding continued. He struggled to throw off the blows, to protect himself, but was unable to get his hands up.

The passage was lost in abysmal darkness. Only half conscious of what he was doing, Jim tried to retreat. But his enemy pursued him, hitting him with jarring blows that left him numb and unfeeling. Finally, he slipped to the deck, even his great strength unable to endure more battering.

A long time later, he fought his way back to consciousness. He was sprawled on the cold steel of the deck, some distance from where he had fallen.

He caught a steampipe housing and pulled himself to a sitting position. His head throbbed with great waves of agony. When he moved, white-hot streaks of pain shot through his brain and something hammered against his skull with great force. He tried to turn his head, and his brain seemed to move like heavy paint in a bucket. A dim light was growing in the east. On the deck he could see the dark smear of his blood where he had been dragged. His attacker had planned to drop him overboard, but had been frightened away, evidently.

Ponga Jim staggered to his feet and reeled against the bulkhead, clutching his throbbing head with both hands. It was caked with blood. Stumbling, he reached the ladder and climbed slowly to the lower bridge. Somehow he got the door open and lunged into his cabin, the roll of the ship sending him sprawling to his knees.

He was still there when the door opened and Brophy came in.

"Skipper, what's happened?" His wide, flat face was incredulous. "What fell on you?"

"I'll get him now," Jim muttered, hardly aware of the other man. "I know how to find him."

For three days Jim stayed in his bunk except when on watch. His face was swollen, and there were cuts and abrasions on the sides of his head. He was remembering that. He had not been struck *over* the head. All the blows had struck *up*. The attacker had struck with peculiar, sidearm blows. It was unusual, and for the average man, unnatural.

His jaw ached, and the back of his head was bruised. However, when he came to the bridge on the fourth day, he was just in time to see the raft.

It was a point on the starboard bow, a crude raft with a man clinging to it. Even as they saw it, the man stirred, trying to rise.

"Pick him up," Jim said, and staggered into the wheelhouse to sit down.

He still sat there when the man was brought to him. Warren and some of the others crowded inside. The man's skull stood out, the skin like thin yellow paper drawn over it. His eyes were blazing pools of fever.

"Ile du Coin," he whispered hoarsely. "Hurry."

"What?" Jim asked. "What's on the Ile du Coin?"

"Sixty men, tortured, starving, dying. Prisoners from a raider. I escaped. They shot, hit me. Hit me." His fingers touched the scalp wound. "Ile du Coin," he muttered again, his wits straying.

131

"How many Nazis?" Jim asked, watching the man narrowly.

He looked up, blinking. "Fifty. A raider sunk, saved the crew. Other ship is due back." He stared at Jim. "They die there, horribly. Please hurry!"

Warren hesitated, looking from the man to Ponga Jim, for once uncertain.

"Might be a trap," he said, hesitantly.

"Yes," Jim said. "But no man looks that bad for a trap."

Aldridge gazed at the man. "We'd better go," he said. "We can get away before the other raider returns." He looked at Ponga Jim. "You know the island?"

"Of course," Jim assured him. "It's one of the Chagos group, not far off our course. We'll go."

The rescued man—his name was Lauren—described the island. Ponga Jim listened and then shook his head.

"A small, rocky island with some scrub and coconut palms? Uninhabited? That's not Ile du Coin. That's Nelson Island. It's in the same group."

Lauren nodded. "The prisoners are in a barbwire stockade beyond a big cluster of palms and well out of sight. The Nazis have a fortified position behind some low dunes and scrubs. You can't see it until you're close by. The cove is too shallow for a ship."

Mayo turned and went below. There was a word or two at Caillaux's cabin, and the door opened.

The general looked at his bandaged head, and Jeanne's eyes widened. "What happened?" she asked.

"Someone tried to get me before I could close the door when I was here last. I got the door shut, and then he tried to kill me."

Briefly, Jim explained. "You see how it is, General. You are my mission. I have no right to risk you or Mademoiselle, yet these men will die if they are not saved."

Caillaux studied Ponga Jim, pulling at his earlobe. Jeanne stepped over to her uncle and took his arm. The general smiled and said, "My niece and I feel the same. You believe you can do this?"

"I do."

"Then the best of luck. We want you to try."

A short time later Ponga Jim studied the island through the glass.

"Half ahead," he said.

Brophy put the engine-room telegraph over and then back to half speed, watching the island.

"We'll drop the hook off the northeastern point," Jim murmured. "The bay has a sandy beach where you can effect a landing. I'll take you and a landing party of Lyssy, Big London, Tupa, Boma, Longboy, and Selim and Sakim.

"The Gunner will have to keep a very sharp lookout for subs and also for the raider."

Warren had come up to the bridge. Wallace and Aldridge were behind him.

"We insist on going," Warren said firmly. "I don't approve of this, but if there are some of our men ashore, we want to help."

"Suit yourself," Jim agreed. "But not all of you. You three can come, and bring five more. Too many men will be worse than none. I want a small party that will maneuver easily. And my men know this sort of fighting."

It wasn't until the prow of the lifeboat grated on the sand that there was any sign of life. Then it was the flash of sunlight on a rifle barrel.

"*Down!*" Jim snapped, and threw himself to the sand. The others flattened instantly, just in time to miss a raking volley.

Instantly, Ponga Jim was on his feet. He made a dozen steps with bullets kicking sand around him and then flattened behind a low hummock and hammered out three quick shots at the spot where he'd seen the rifle. There was a gasping cry and then silence.

No orders were necessary. The flyers hesitated and then took their cue from Lyssy and the crew of the *Semiramis*. They worked their way forward, keeping to shallow places and losing their bodies in the sand.

Jim touched Lyssy. "They are bunched right ahead of us. Slip over to the left and flank them. London, you take the right. Take no chances, and keep your fire down. I want them out of that position."

The two men disappeared, and Mayo looked at Warren. "This is war, friend," he said grimly.

The Nazis opened a hot fire that swept the dunes, a searching volley that covered the ground thoroughly.

Only the hollows saved the landing party.

Mayo scooped sand away and worked his body forward. A shot kicked sand into his face. He worked in behind a low bush and lifted his head slowly beside it.

He had been right. The low dunes behind which the Nazis were concealed ran across the island diagonally, but both flanks were exposed. He snapped a quick shot into the space ahead and then slid back in time to miss the answering volley.

The Nazis were shooting steadily, hammering each available screen with steady fire. But suddenly a rifle cracked off to the left, and there was a scream of pain. The rifle spoke again, and there was an answering volley. Another shot came from the right, and Jim yelled.

In a scattered line his men rushed forward firing from all positions. The Germans, although superior in numbers, retreated hastily. Ponga Jim stopped, braced himself, and fired. A Nazi stumbled and fell headlong. Two more were down in the hollow where they had taken shelter. Now another stumbled and collapsed as a bullet ripped into his body.

Jenkins, a flyer from Kalgoorlie, rushed up beside Jim, stopped suddenly, and dropped to his face in the sand.

Jim fired. The Nazi let his rifle slip from his hands, bowed his head and took two steps, and then toppled.

Mayo crawled behind a five-foot bank of sand and looked around. All of Warren's pomposity was gone. Under fire, the man had changed. Whatever else he was, he came of fighting stock.

Ring Wallace, an old hand at this game, was grinning. "Nice work, pal. Now what?"

"We're stuck," Jim said. "They've got a fortified position up there, and it will be tough to get them out of it. Listen to those machine guns. Those boys know their stuff, too."

Brophy had been grazed by a bullet, and Tupa had a flesh wound. Aside from the first flyer, there were no serious injuries.

Wallace nodded to Jim's comment. "Yeah, I could see the edge of a concrete abutment. It's in crescent form and backed by the cove."

"Let's rush them," Warren said. "Otherwise it's a stalemate until that raider gets back."

Ponga Jim shook his head. "We'd lose men in a rush. Wars aren't won with dead soldiers. There's always a way to take a position without losing many men, if you look for it." Suddenly his eyes narrowed. "Slug, do you recall what the chart said about the water in that cove?"

Brophy nodded. "There's a coral ledge topped with sand with about a fathom of water over it. Outside of that it slopes off gradually until at a hundred yards it's about three fathoms. Why?"

"You'll be in command here. I'll take Selim, Longboy, and Sakim with me. We'll bring the wounded aboard. Now scatter out and don't move either forward or back, get me?"

"What are you going to do?" Warren protested.

"Wait and see," Jim said. "If this works I'm one up on the Nazis for trying new angles. We're going to take that position in less than thirty minutes! Now listen. Keep up an intermittent fire. Pretty soon Millan will lay five shells in that fort, get me? Then you'll hear shooting over there. And when you hear shooting beyond the wall, come running. I'll need help."

Millan met them at the ladder. "What's up?" he demanded.

Jim indicated the cove.

"As the fort lays, the situation is impregnable from the island with our weapons. I want you to lay five shells behind that abutment. And they've got to be right on the spot. If you overshoot, you'll kill the prisoners. If you undershoot, you'll get our boys for sure."

The Gunner studied the situation. Then he rolled his chewing tobacco in his jaw and spat.

"Yeah," he said, "I'll lay 'em right in their laps."

"Well, whatever you do," Ponga Jim added, "don't drop any shells in the cove, because if you do they'll be in my lap!"

"The cove?" Millan was incredulous. "You couldn't get in there with a boat! They'd riddle you!"

Ponga Jim grinned. "Break out those Momsen lungs, will you? I'll show those Jerries some tricks!"

An hour dragged by. The warm afternoon sun baked down on the little island. Ring Wallace took a swallow from his canteen and swore. Warren wiped the sweat from his face and kept his hands away from the hot rifle barrel. "I wonder what became of Mayo?" he asked.

"Darned if I know," Ring said. "But he's got something up his sleeve. Whatever it is, it better be good. That raider has me worried."

A gun crashed from the *Semiramis*, and a shell screeched overhead, bursting beyond the abutment with a terrific concussion. A fountain of sand lifted into the air. Another shell screeched, and there was another explosion.

"That Millan!" Brophy said admiringly. "That guy can put a shell in your pocket. Just name the pocket!"

Two more shells dropped beyond the abutment, then a fifth.

The water of the cove stirred and rippled. Up from the pondlike surface five weird heads appeared, five faces masked in Momsen lungs. Lowering themselves into the water beyond the point, they had walked around in ten feet of water. Now they stripped the waterproof jackets from their guns and walked on. They were within a hundred feet of the shore, in just four feet of water, before they were seen.

One machine gun emplacement had been smashed to bits

with the first shell. Two others had exploded on the abutment itself, and a third had landed in a gasoline supply that was burning furiously. The final shell had been shrapnel, and the devastation had been terrific. Seven men had fallen from that one shell alone.

Crawling from behind a pile of boxes, one of the defenders glanced at the cove. His jaw dropped. For a fatal second he stared, uncomprehending; then he jerked up his rifle. Too late. Ponga Jim shot him in the stomach. As the startled defenders turned, Jim ran up the last few feet, and his Luger automatic opened with a roar like a machine gun.

In a scattered line the other men rushed up the beach. The Germans, caught off balance, were rattled. They fell back. And in that instant the frontal attack broke over them. Brophy, Wallace, Warren, and the others cleared the barrier. The two sides met in a deadly rush.

A German dove at Jim. He spun out of the way, clouting the man over the head with the barrel of his gun. Then he snapped a quick shot at a man leveling a rifle at Wallace and fired a burst into a group trying to swing the machine gun on the prisoners.

A terrific blow struck him over the ear, and he went down, grabbing at the man's legs. He upset his assailant and scrambled astride, swinging both hands for the fellow's jaw. Then he was on his feet again and grabbing up a rifle. He jerked the barrel up into a charging German's stomach and pulled the trigger. The man's mouth fell open, and with his back half blown away, he sagged limply to the ground.

As suddenly as it had started, it was over. Brophy released the prisoners, and Wallace herded the half-dozen Nazis still alive into a corner of the fort where Lyssy and Big London took them over.

Aldridge came up on the run.

"Nice going!" he said, clapping Mayo on the shoulder. "That

attack from the rear from under water completely demoralized them."

"Yeah," Wallace agreed. "Now if we only had the spy—"

"We have," Ponga Jim said shortly.

A silence fell over the crowd. Brophy's gun slipped into his hand, and he backed off a little, covering the group. Colonel Warren looked from one to the other, puzzled.

"What's the matter with your shoulder, Aldridge?" Jim said, unexpectedly. "Hurt it?"

"Oh, that?" Aldridge shrugged. "Years ago. Can't lift my arm overhead. But what about this spy?"

"So when you hit a man," Mayo continued, "you couldn't hit him over the head? It would have to be a swinging, sidearm motion? Then you were the guy who jumped me in the passage."

Aldridge smiled, but his eyes were cold, wary.

"Nonsense! You think I'm a spy? Me? I went to school with Warren, there, and—"

"Remember the first day I saw you?" Mayo said. "You mentioned the Qasavara affair. That business is lost in the files of the British Intelligence service. My own connection with it is known to only two Englishmen—Colonel Sutherland and Major Arnold, who were with me. If you knew of it, you had to learn from a Nazi source."

Mayo smiled. "I was suspicious of you for knowing that. Later, I checked on the location of the flyers during my attack. You could have been in your hammock. On the other hand, you could have slipped out. From the locations, no one else could have.

"So today I had you followed by Fly Johnny, one of my crew. In fact, for the past week he has never been more than a few feet from you.

"Today, when we first came ashore, Millan went through your quarters. He found the package of flashlight powder you used in making signals. He also found other evidence, so I think the case is clear."

Aldridge nodded, his face hard.

"Sounds conclusive," he agreed, "so I guess—"

He wheeled like a cat and jerked Warren's gun from his hand. Eyes blazing with hatred, the gun swept up. But he was too slow. Ponga Jim stepped forward in one quick stride, half turning on the ball of his foot. His right fist smashed upward in an uppercut that slammed Aldridge into the sand, the gun flying from his fingers.

Ponga Jim looked at him once. "Bring him along," he said, "we'll be going now."

"You know," Warren said seriously, "the more I think about it the more I believe Drake had something!"

Ponga Jim grinned. "Yeah, and he would have liked you!"

In the radio shack, Ponga Jim Mayo picked up the stub of a pencil, grinned, and scratched out a message.

MAJOR WILLIAM ARNOLD
RAFFLES HOTEL
SINGAPORE, S. I.

PROCEEDED WITH CAUTION AND A LOT OF GOOD IT DID. ARMED MERCHANTMAN OF TEN THOUSAND TONS NOW HAS HOLE IN HIS BOW AND DISABLED GUN. WE HAVE ENEMY AGENT ABOARD—IN IRONS. WE HAVE MET THE ENEMY AND YOU CAN HAVE THEM. WILL BE IN RED SEA FRIDAY. NUTS TO YOU.

MAYO.

AUTHOR'S NOTE

THE RED SEA

The Red Sea is about 1,200 miles long and at its widest point, 190 miles. Although there are dangerous coral reefs along the shores, the waters in the main channel are deep. During the latter days of Egyptian control and in Roman times, ships sailed from Red Sea ports to India at the rate of one per day, or about 120 ships per year during the sailing season. These ports, Myos, Hormos, Berenice, and Ptolemais Theron, are now silted up and no longer in use. There are a few foundations remaining and some evidence of what once existed there.

Long before the Suez Canal was more than a dream, there had been a canal dug by order of the pharaohs to connect the Nile with the Red Sea. Most of it has since been filled with sand as a result of the constant winds.

At the north the sea is divided into the Gulf of Suez, leading to the canal, and the Gulf of Aqaba. The Sinai Peninsula lies between them, on which is the Mount Sinai of the Bible, also known as Jebel Musa. It is 7,450 feet high.

SOUTH OF SUEZ

CHAPTER I
Strange Battlewagon

The heavy concussion of the first shell brought Ponga Jim
Mayo out of his bunk, wide-awake in an instant. He was
pulling on his shoes when he heard the whistle in the speaking
tube.

"Skipper?" It was Gunner Millan. "We're running into a
battle! Can't see a thing but red flashes yet, about three points
on the starboard bow. Sounds like a battlewagon."

"Put her over to port about four degrees," Ponga Jim said
quietly. "Have the watch call Brophy and get the gun crews
topside."

He got up, slid into his dungarees, and slipped on the
shoulder holster with the forty-five Colt. There would be no
need for it at sea, but he had worn the gun so long he felt
undressed without it.

When Ponga Jim reached the bridge the sky was lit with an
angry glow of flame. Two freighters of the convoy off to the
starboard were afire, and something was lifted toward the sky
that looked like the stern of a sinking ship. They could hear the
steady fire of six-inch guns and then the heavy boom of something much bigger.

*   *   *

Second mate Millan came toward him along the bridge, swearing under his breath.

"Skipper," he said. "I must be nuts, but I'd swear that gun wasn't smaller than an eighteen-inch, and there's nothing afloat carries a gun that big!"

"Sounds like it," Jim said briefly. "Might be a sixteen. The *Tirpitz*, maybe. But you wouldn't think they'd gamble a battleship in waters as narrow as the Red Sea."

The blazing wreck of one freighter was directly opposite them, and suddenly a low, ominous blackness moved between them and the blazing ship. For a few minutes it was clearly outlined against the red glow of flame.

Squat, black, and ugly, the monster glistened in the reddish light. It was built low and completely covered by what appeared to be a steel shell. Even as they looked they saw the muzzle of a heavy gun belch flame. A big freighter, almost a mile away, was attempting to escape. Even as they watched, the shell struck it amidships.

Suddenly, but with every move so perfectly detailed as to seem like a slow-motion picture, the distant freighter burst. The amidships vanished and the bow and stern seemed to lift away from it and then fell back into the flame-tinged water. Then there was a slow rain of black debris.

"Gun crews standing by, sir," first mate Slug Brophy said, as he came up. He saluted snappily, but he was scowling as he looked off across the water. "What the devil kind of a craft *is* *that?*" he demanded. "Looks like she was a seagoing tank."

Ponga Jim nodded. "It's what I've been wondering why someone didn't do," he said crisply. "That's a new battleship. No elaborate superstructure, no basket masts or turrets. She's completely covered by a steel shell and probably bomb-proof. She's built along the lines of a streamlined Merrimac."

"Lucky that fire's in her eyes and we're back here," Slug said. "One shell from her and we'd be blown so high we'd starve to death falling back."

"Yeah." Jim studied the warship through his glass and then glanced ahead. "Gunner, lay all five guns on that baby. I'm going to give her a broadside and then run for it."

"You're nuts!" Brophy exploded. "Why, Chief—"

"You heard me," Ponga Jim said sharply. "Get going."

He stepped into the wheelhouse.

"Selim," he said to the pockmarked, knife-scarred man at the wheel, "aren't we abreast of the old smuggler's passage through the reef? It gives us about five fathoms, doesn't it?"

Selim nodded, lifting his eyes from the compass.

"I take her through?" he asked.

Ponga Jim studied the mystery ship ahead thoughtfully and then the nearing bulk of a large rocky island.

"Yeah," he said. "We'll fire that barge a broadside and then slip around that island and through the reef passage. They can't follow us, and blacked out the way they have us these days, we'll be invisible against that rocky shore. We got a chance."

He stepped back to the bridge and lifted his megaphone.

"You may fire when ready, Gridley!" he said and grinned.

The crash of the five 5.9s left his ears momentarily dead and empty. The freighter heeled sharply over. With his glasses on the warship, Ponga Jim waited for the *Semiramis* to recover.

"All right, Gunner," he called. "Once more!"

He had his glasses on the warship when the salvo struck. He scowled and then spun on his heel.

"Hard over!" he snapped crisply. "Show them our stern, if anything." He stepped on the speaking tube. "Chief," he called, "give me all she's got! I don't want to use the telegraph. Jangles too much. We're in a spot, so keep her rolling."

Slug Brophy and Gunner Millan had returned to the bridge. The squat first mate wiped his face with a blue handkerchief.

"You sure pick 'em big when you want trouble!" he observed. "See those five-point-nines slide off that shell? Like rice off a turtle's back! What kind of a ship is that, anyway?"

"That ship," Ponga Jim said quietly, "can destroy British and American naval supremacy! The United States has the biggest,

145

best, and most efficient navy afloat, but we haven't anything as invulnerable to attack as that ship!"

Behind them a gun boomed, and off to the left a huge geyser of water lifted toward the sky. Ponga Jim glanced aft and then looked at the black bulk of the rocky island. Selim was cutting it close, but no one knew the Red Sea better than he did.

The *Semiramis* steamed straight ahead and then at a low word from Selim, slowed to half speed as he turned the ship at right angles to her course. Ponga Jim stared into the darkness ahead, hearing the roll of the surf on the coral reef. He put his hand up to his forehead, to find he was sweating.

Brophy stood close beside him, staring down at the black, froth-fringed reef dead ahead.

"You sure this guy knows what he's doing?" Slug muttered. "If he doesn't—"

"He does," Mayo said quietly. "Selim was a smuggler in this sea for several years. He knows every cove and passage in the eleven hundred miles of it."

As if to prove his statement, the reef suddenly seemed to open before them, and an opening, invisible until they were close up, appeared in the reef.

In a matter of seconds they were through and in the clear water of the inside passage. . . .

Two days later the *Semiramis* steamed slowly into the harbor at Port Tewfik and moved up to the place at the dock that had been made ready for them.

"Mr. Brophy"—Ponga Jim turned to the chief mate—"get the hatches off and the cargo out of her as quick as you can. Take nothing from anybody, use any gear you need, but it must get out. Also, I want a man at the gangway every hour of the day and night. Nobody comes aboard or leaves without my permission. Also, I want one man forward and one aft. All to be armed. Understand?"

"You must be expecting trouble," a cool voice suggested.

Ponga Jim turned to find himself facing a square-shouldered

young man with a blond mustache and humorous blue eyes. He was a slender man with a narrow face, dark, immaculate, and with a military bearing, and had just boarded the *Semiramis* with a companion.

"William!" he exclaimed. "What in time are you doing in Egypt? Thought you were in Singapore?"

Major William Arnold shrugged his shoulders.

"Trouble here, too," he said. "Heard you were coming in, so thought I'd drop down and see you." His gaze sharpened. "Have any trouble coming up from Aden?"

"We didn't," Ponga Jim said drily, "but we saw a convoy get smashed to hell."

"You *saw* it?"

Ponga Jim was nodding as Major Arnold quickly added:

"Jim, let me present Nathan Demarest, our former attaché at Bucharest. He's working with me on this job."

"Glad to know you," Ponga Jim said, and then he looked back at Arnold. "Yes, we saw it," he said briefly, and went on, as his glance went back to Demarest. "Arnold will tell you that I don't run to convoys, so we were traveling alone. About six bells in the middle watch I got a call and got on deck to find a big warship blasting the daylights out of the convoy. Only one destroyer remained in action when we came up to them. And that not for long."

"A ship?" Arnold demanded. "Not submarines?"

"A ship," Mayo repeated. "A ship that couldn't have been less than forty thousand tons. She was streamlined and completely shelled over like a floating fort, and she mounted eighteen-inch guns."

"Your friend Captain Mayo is a humorist," Demarest suggested to Arnold, smiling. "There is no such ship."

"I'm not joking," Ponga Jim said stiffly. "There was such a ship, and we saw it."

Arnold looked at his friend thoughtfully.

"What happened, Jim?" he finally asked.

147

"We were coming up in the darkness and were unseen. I gave them two salvos from my guns, and then we slipped around an island and got away."

"You hit her?"

"Yes—direct hits—and they didn't even shake her. Just like shooting at a tank with a target rifle."

Demarest's face had hardened. "If this is true we must get in touch with the Admiralty," he said. "Such a ship must be run down at once."

"If you'll take my word for it," Mayo said slowly, "I'd advise being careful. This ship is something new. I don't believe bombs would have any effect on her at all. She looks like another secret weapon."

Ponga Jim Mayo glanced at the winches.

The booms were being rigged, and in a few minutes the cargo would be coming out of the freighter.

"Is this what brought you here, William?" he asked. "Or something else?"

"Something else," the major said. "Have you heard of Carter's death? Ambrose Carter, the munitions man? He was found shot to death in his apartment near Shepheard's in Cairo three weeks ago. Then General McKnight was poisoned, and Colonel Norfolk of the CID, who was investigating, was stabbed."

"McKnight poisoned?" Ponga Jim exclaimed. "I heard he died of heart failure."

"That's our story," Arnold agreed. "We mustn't allow anyone to know, Jim. But those are only three of the deaths. There have been nine others, all of key men. Some poisoned, some shot, one stabbed, two found dead without any evidence of cause of death, others drowned, strangled, or snake bit."

"Snake bit?"

"By an Indian cobra. The thing had been coiled in one man's bed. When it bit him he died before help could get to him. Jim, they called me here because these deaths can't be explained. Carter, for instance, was an acknowledged pro-Nazi, a former friend of Hitler's. If it weren't for that, it would seem logical the Nazis were starting a reign of terror, killing off the leadership for a major attack in the Near East."

"If not the Nazis," Jim protested, "then who could it be?"

"I wish I knew." Arnold's eyes narrowed. "But you'd better come along and tell this to Skelton. He's in charge here in Port Tewfik. The man who will have to know and to act."

CHAPTER II
Death Strikes the Semiramis

Seated in the office of Anthony Skelton, two hours later, Ponga Jim Mayo repeated his story, quietly and in detail. Two other men were there besides Demarest and Arnold. One he was introduced to as Captain Woodbern, of the Navy. The other was General Jerome Kernan.

Before Ponga Jim's story was completed, Skelton was tapping his desk impatiently. Captain Woodbern was frankly smiling.

"Major Arnold," Skelton said abruptly, "I've heard a great deal of your ability. I've also heard of the work Captain Mayo has been doing in the Far East. Which makes me the more surprised at your taking our time, Major, with such an obvious cock-and-bull story. This Captain Mayo evidently has a peculiar sense of humor or is susceptible to hallucinations. Such a story as his is preposterous on the face of it!"

Arnold stiffened. "I know Captain Mayo too well, Mr. Skelton," he replied stiffly, "to doubt his word. If he says this story is true, then I believe it is true!"

"Then you're more credulous than any intelligence officer should be!" Skelton snapped.

"Captain Mayo evidently saw something," Captain Woodbern said, smiling, "but I'm afraid the darkness, the battle, the flames, and the general excitement caused his imagination to work a little overtime."

General Kernan turned slightly in his chair. He was a big man with a hard jaw, a cold eye, and a close-clipped mustache.

"Mayo isn't the type to be seeing things, Skelton," he said. "Major Arnold has known him for some time, and his work has been valuable. I want to hear more of his story."

Skelton glanced down at some papers on his desk. "We'll see that proper investigation is made," he said shortly. "In fact, we have already ordered two destroyers to the scene."

Ponga Jim leaned forward. "Then, Mr. Skelton," he said quietly, "you've sent two destroyers to destruction. Either they will return having found nothing, or they'll never come back." He got up abruptly. "Thanks for believing my story, General. As for you, Skelton, I'm not in the habit of having my word questioned. All I can say or do about that here and now is to assure you that you are following the same trail of incompetence and smugness of others who didn't believe Hitler would attack Britain, did not believe in parachute troops, or that the Japanese would bomb Pearl Harbor and the Philippines while suing for peace. Well, do what you choose. I shall investigate further myself!"

Skelton's eyes blazed.

"No," he said sharply, "you won't! In the Far East your blunderings may have been occasionally convenient, but we want no civilian interference here. You make one move to investigate or to interfere and I'll have the *Semiramis* interned for the duration!"

Ponga Jim smiled suddenly. He leaned his big brown fists on the edge of the desk and looked into Skelton's eyes.

"Listen, pal," he said coldly, "you may have a lot of red tape around the throats of other better men than you. But I'm not subject to your orders, and I'll sail when and where I please. If you want to intern my ship, I've got five-point-nines and plenty of ammunition. You'll think you've tackled something. When I get ready to sail, I'm sailing. Stop me if you feel lucky."

He glanced at Arnold, whose face was white.

"Sorry, William, but you can't help that. Be seeing you." He strode from the room.

Skelton's face was deathly white. "I want that man put under arrest and his ship interned!" he snapped.

General Kernan got to his feet.

"You're starting something with the wrong man, Skelton," he said smoothly. "If necessary, Captain Mayo would shoot his way out of harbor or sink trying."

"Nonsense!" Skelton snapped.

"No." Kernan was looking after Mayo thoughtfully. "The man's a Yank, but I was doubting if they had any left like him. Now that I know they have, I feel a lot better. Mayo's another of the school of Perry, Farragut, Decatur, and Hull."

Nathan Demarest left the room quietly, glanced down the hall along which Mayo had gone, and then stepped into an empty office and picked up the telephone.

Ponga Jim walked swiftly down the street and then stopped in a place for a drink. When he turned to leave, he saw a slim, wiry man sitting at a table near the door. The man did not look up, but something in the man's attitude made Mayo suspicious. He would almost have sworn it was the same man he had seen loitering outside Skelton's office as he left. He scowled. Who would want him followed in Suez?

The quay was a litter of piled barrels and cases, of gear and bales. Ponga Jim was just passing a huge crane whose bulk forced him to the edge of the dock, when a black body catapulted from the darkness and smashed him with a shoulder, just hip high. He felt himself falling and grabbed desperately, catching his attacker by the arm. They fell, plunging into the black water with terrific force, but even as they sank Ponga Jim felt his attacker's arm slip from his grasp, and the next instant the man had drawn a knife and lunged toward him.

Ponga Jim dived and felt the hot blade of the knife along his shoulder. His lungs all but bursting, he slammed a punch into the man's belly. He saw his attacker's mouth open, but the man was a veritable fiend, and he lunged again with the knife, teeth bared. Ponga Jim pushed away, kicking the man in the belly. Then they broke water.

Instantly, the fellow took a breath and dived, but Ponga Jim went down with him. At one time Ponga Jim had been a skin diver for pearls. The swift thought flashed now that this fellow was good, and he had a knife, but—

The man swung in the water, his body as slippery as an eel's, and then he lunged at Ponga Jim with the knife. But Mayo was too fast. He dived again, catching the man's wrist. Turning the arm, he jerked it down across his shoulder with terrific force.

Then he pulled free, smashing a fist into the fellow's belly for luck. As he swam he could see the man sinking, his teeth bared, his mouth leaving a trail of bubbles. The arm was broken.

Ponga Jim swam to a small boat dock and scrambled from the water. For a moment he stood there, dripping and staring back, but there was nothing to be seen. He put his hand up, and it came away from his shoulder bloody.

"Somebody," he muttered softly, "doesn't like me!"

The dark shape of the *Semiramis* loomed not fifty feet away. He climbed the ladder to the dock and then moved warily toward the freighter. As he came up the gangway, a dark shape materialized from beside the hatch. He recognized the half-shaven head of the big Toradjas, one of his trusted crew.

"It's all right, Lyssy," he said. "It's me."

"Something happen astern, Captain. Somebody—" Lyssy saw Ponga Jim's dripping clothes, and his eyes widened. "Somebody try to kill you?"

"That's right." Mayo glanced back at the dock. "Keep your eyes open. Who else is on watch?"

"Big London, he forward. Longboy aft. Sakim, he around somewhere, too."

"Has anyone been here?"

"Yes, Captain. One man he come say he want to talk to you. He say very important. He say General Kernan send him."

"Where is he?" Ponga Jim demanded.

152

"In your cabin. You say no man come aboard, this man he worry to see you. We lock him in."

Ponga Jim grinned. "Okay. You stay here."

He quickly climbed the ladder to his deck and then fitted his key in the lock of his door. He swung it open—and stopped dead in his tracks. The man sitting in Ponga Jim's favorite chair, facing the door, had been shot above the left eyebrow.

Slowly, Ponga Jim reached behind him and drew the door to. He circled the body, studying it with narrowed eyes. Then he stepped behind the body and sighted across the dead man's head in line with the wound. The bullet had come through the open porthole. In line with the port was the corner of the warehouse roof. Whoever had fired the shot had stood on that corner and made a perfect job.

Ponga Jim went out to the deck and called Lyssy.

"Did you hear a shot?" he demanded.

"No, Captain, nobody shoot!" Lyssy said positively.

That meant one thing to Ponga Jim. A silencer had been used.

"The man up there is dead," he said. "He was shot from that warehouse roof."

Sakim came up, and Ponga Jim hurriedly scratched a note.

"Take this message to Major Arnold at this address," he instructed. "Give it to no one else. Then return here."

He went back into his cabin and, closing the door, careful not to disturb the position of the body, he searched the murdered man's pockets. He spread everything he found on his desk and studied the collection carefully. There was a key ring with several keys, a billfold, a fountain pen, a gun, some odd change, mostly silver, and a ticket stub indicating that the victim had but recently arrived from Alexandria. Also, there was a magnificent emerald ring, the gem being carved in the form of a scarab.

Turning his attention to the billfold, Ponga Jim found a packet of money amounting to about eighty Egyptian pounds, around four hundred dollars. In one pocket of the billfold was a white card and on it, in neat handwriting, a name.

ZARA HAMMEDAN

After a few minutes thought, he pocketed the key ring, the card with the name, and the emerald ring. On second thought, he returned the ring to the table, retaining the other things he had chosen.

CHAPTER III
Too Late!

At a sudden rap on the door, Ponga Jim looked up. He opened the door to find Major Arnold, General Kernan, and Nathan Demarest awaiting him. They had come promptly in answer to Mayo's note.

Arnold crossed at once to the body and made a cursory examination.

"Then this man who has been killed never managed to talk to you?" General Kernan asked.

"No," Ponga Jim replied. "I was delayed myself. Someone tried to add me to your list of killings."

Arnold looked up quickly. "I noticed you were wet. Did they shove you in?"

Ponga Jim nodded. He was looking across the room at a mirror.

"Yes. Good attempt, too. But I don't kill very easy."

"What happened?" Demarest asked. "Did you—catch him?"

"No. I killed him. He cut me a little, but not much."

"But you were in the water," Demarest persisted. "How could you kill him?"

"I killed him," Ponga Jim said quietly, "in the water. He got his belly and lungs full of it."

Demarest's eyes narrowed a little, and then he glanced at the body. "That man was a half-caste," he said. "But his killers must have taken him for you."

"I don't think so," Ponga Jim said. "I think the killer knew who he was shooting."

"So do I," Kernan said. "This man who was shot came here with a message for you. He came to me first, learned you were here, and said he would talk to no one but you. Had some message for you."

Arnold straightened up. "Had you noticed something, Jim? No identification on this man. Not a thing. We can check on this ticket stub and the gun, but I'm sure they will give us nothing."

"What about the ring?" Ponga Jim asked.

"Old, isn't it?" Arnold said. "And odd looking. It might be a clue."

Ponga Jim picked up the ring. "Look at that again, William. Emeralds and rubies were carved into scarabs only for royalty. The emerald itself is big, the ring too heavy for ordinary wear. It's probably a funeral ring, and probably dates back three thousand years. That ring is museum stuff. But I'll bet it didn't come from any museum."

"Why?" General Kernan asked. He examined the ring curiously.

"Such prize archaeological specimens are too well cared for. And if anything as valuable as that were lost, everyone would have heard of it. No, this man, whoever he was, had found a tomb and had been looting it."

"He might have picked it up in some thieves' market," Demarest protested.

"What I'm wondering," Arnold said, "is how all this can tie in with your mysterious battleship? A thief with a stolen ring or one looted from a tomb could scarcely have anything to do with such a thing."

"That battleship," Ponga Jim suggested, "or even if I was

crazy and it was only a submarine or two, must have a base. The first problem, it seems to me, is to locate that base. The fact that the ship is in the Red Sea gives us a chance to keep it here—if we can. My theory is that this dead guy may have known where the base is, and maybe that knowledge ties in with that ring."

Major Arnold stayed on after the others had gone.

"Go slow, Jim," he advised. "Skelton doesn't approve of civilians interfering in government affairs, and he persists in maintaining that you have no right to have an armed ship, that actually you're a pirate."

"Yeah?" Ponga Jim chuckled. "Maybe he's right. I'm an American, even though I've spent little time there. My shipping business is in war areas but I'm not asking America's protection. I protect myself. But seriously, William, this business has got me going in circles. Why the rush to kill me? Who knows, except you guys, that I saw that warship? Who knows that a shipowner and skipper like myself would ever dream of investigating the thing? Why should this guy with the ring come to me?"

Arnold nodded. "I've thought of that," he said. "Frankly, Jim, other people have, too. Skelton even hinted that you might have sunk that convoy."

"*What?*" Ponga Jim's face hardened. "Some day that guy's going to make me sore."

"But see his angle. You have guns. There were two destroyers with that convoy, but what would prevent you from giving one of them a salvo at close quarters when they expected nothing of the kind? And then the other?"

"There's something in that," Ponga Jim admitted. "But you and I know it's baloney. And where does this killing me come in? Only one way I can see it. These babies have an espionage system that reaches right to the top here in Egypt. They know about me coming through; they know about my plan to go on."

Arnold was thoughtful. "Jim," he said slowly, "I've got a

hunch. You've knocked around a lot. Suppose you were right, and this isn't a Nazi deal? Who or what could it be? My hunch is that you know, and somebody knows you know, and is afraid you might talk."

Ponga Jim frowned. "I know? What d'you mean?"

"Suppose that while knocking around—you used to be in Africa—you stumbled across some person or place connected with this. You have forgotten, but someone in this plot hasn't."

Mayo nodded. "Might be something to it. But what?"

"Think it over. In the meanwhile, we'll have this body taken off your hands."

When Arnold had gone Ponga Jim walked out on deck and called Selim and Sakim.

"Listen," he said. "You boys used to be wise to everything that happened in the Red Sea. I want you to go out into the bazaars, anywhere, and I want the gossip. I want to know more about this warship we saw. I want to know about the guy that was killed in my cabin. Above all, I want to know something about a woman named Zara Hammedan!"

The two Afridis stiffened.

"Who, Nakhoda?" Selim said. "Did you say Zara Hammedan?"

"That's right."

"But, Nakhoda, we know who she is!" Selim hesitated. Then: "I will tell you, Nakhoda. This is a secret among Moslems, but you are our protector and friend. There is among Moslems a young movement, a sect of those who are fanatics who would draw together all Moslem countries in a huge empire. These men have chosen Zara Hammedan for their spiritual leader. She is scarcely more than a girl, Nakhoda, but she is of amazing beauty."

"Who is she? An Arab?"

Selim shrugged. "Perhaps. It is said she is of the family of the Sultan of Kishin, leader of the powerful Mahra tribe, whose territory extends along the coast from Museinaa to Damkut."

Slug Brophy came up as the two were leaving.

"Any orders, Skipper? We'll have her empty an hour after daybreak."

"Yeah."

Ponga Jim talked slowly for several minutes, and Slug nodded.

"Can you swing it?" he asked finally.

"Sure." Brophy hitched up his trousers. "This is going to be good. . . ."

A few minutes after daybreak, Ponga Jim went ashore and headed for Golmar Street. As he disappeared, Brophy stepped out on deck. With him was Big London.

"That's the lay," Slug said briefly. "The chief's going alone. You follow him, see? But keep that ugly mug of yours out of sight. I got a hunch he's sticking his neck out, and I want you close by if he does. He'd raise the roof if he knew it, so keep your head down."

The giant black man nodded eagerly and then went ashore. Brophy looked after him, grinning.

"Well, Skipper," he muttered, "if you do get into it, you can use that guy."

For three hours, Ponga Jim was busy. He dropped into various bars, consumed a few drinks, ate breakfast, and lounged about. In his white-topped peaked cap with its captain's insignia, his faded khaki suit, and woven-leather sandals, he was not conspicuous. Only the unusual breadth of his shoulders and his sun-browned face somehow stood out. The bulge under his left shoulder was barely noticeable.

The streets of Suez were jammed. War had brought prosperity to the port, and the ships that came up from around the Cape of Good Hope were mostly docking here. Hundreds of soldiers were about the streets. Ghurkas, Sikhs, and Punjabis from India, stalwart Australians and New Zealanders, occasional Scotsmen, and a number of R.A.F. flyers. And there were seamen from all the seven seas, thronging ashore for a night or a day and then off to sea again. There was a stirring in the bazaars, and rumors were rife of new activity in Libya, of fighting to break out in Iraq once more, of German aggression in Turkey.

And the grapevine of the Orient was at work, with stories from all the Near East drifting here. To a man who knew his way around, things were to be learned in the bazaars.

Ponga Jim went on to Port Said, flying over and later flying back. At four in the afternoon, he presented himself at Skelton's office.

He was admitted at once. Demarest, Kernan, Arnold, Woodbern, and Skelton himself were there.

"Glad you dropped in, Mayo," Skelton said abruptly. "I was about to send for you. Our destroyers wirelessed that they could find only wreckage. Two more destroyers coming up from Aden effected a junction with the same report. What have you to say to that?"

"The warship could have hidden," Ponga Jim said quietly. "You would scarcely expect it to wait for you."

"Hidden? In the Red Sea?" Skelton smiled coldly. "Captain Mayo, a warship could not be concealed in the Red Sea. No ship could be."

"No?" Ponga Jim smiled in turn.

"No," Skelton said. "Furthermore, Captain Mayo, I have deemed it wise to order your ship interned until we can investigate further. I am a little curious as to those guns you carry. I also hear you carry a pocket submarine and an amphibian plane. Strange equipment for an honest freighter."

"The spoils of war," Mayo assured him, still smiling. "I captured them and have found them of use. And I hate to disappoint you, Skelton, but I'm afraid if you expect to intern the *Semiramis* you are a bit late."

"What do you mean?" Skelton snapped.

"The *Semiramis*," Ponga Jim said softly, "finished discharging shortly after daybreak this morning. She left port immediately!"

"*What!*"

Skelton was on his feet, his face white with anger. The other men tensed. But out of the corner of his eye, Ponga Jim could see a twinkle in General Kernan's eyes.

"No doubt you'll find the *Semiramis*," Ponga Jim said coolly, "since you say no ship can be concealed in the Red Sea. Good hunting, Skelton!"

He turned and started for the door.

A buzzer sounded, and behind him he heard Skelton lift the phone.

"What?" Skelton shouted. "Both of them?" The telephone dropped back into the cradle. "Gentlemen," Skelton said sharply, "the destroyers sent from this base to investigate Captain Mayo's report have both been sunk. A partial message was received, telling how they had been attacked. Captain Mayo, you are under arrest!"

"Sorry, gentlemen," Mayo said, "but I can't wait!"

He swung the door open and sprang into the hall.

"Stop him!" Skelton roared.

A burly soldier leaped from his position by the wall, grabbing at Mayo with both hands. Ponga Jim grabbed the big man by the wrist and hurled him over his back in a flying mare that sent the big fellow crashing into the opposite wall. Then he was down the hall, out into the street, and with one jump, was into the crowd.

Another soldier rushed from the building and started down the steps close on Ponga Jim's heels. A Herculean black man, lounging near the door, deftly thrust his foot in the way, and the soldier spilled head over heels into the crowd at the foot of the stone steps.

Rounding a corner, Ponga Jim slipped into a crowded bazaar. He stopped briefly at a stall, and when he left he was wrapped in a long Arab cloak, or aba, and on his head was a headcloth bound with an aghal. With his dark skin and his black hair he looked like a native.

He walked on, mingling with the people of the bazaar. Twice soldiers passed him, their eyes scanning the bazaar, but none looked at him.

But as Ponga Jim drifted slowly from the bazaar and out into the less crowded streets, a slim, hawk-featured man was close

160

behind. And a little further back, Big London, his mighty muscles concealed by his own aba, trailed along, watching with jungle-trained cunning the two men in the crowd ahead.

CHAPTER IV
Zara Hammedan

The marketplaces of the East teem with gossip, and stories are told over the buying of leather or the selling of fruit or in the harems.

To hear them, many an intelligence officer would pay a full year's salary.

During the morning, Ponga Jim had heard much. Now, in his simple disguise and with his easy, natural flow of Arabic, he heard more. A discreet comment or two added to his information.

Several points held his interest. If the Nazis were behind the mysterious killings of the key men who had been murdered here, and if they owned the mystery warship, why had Ambrose Carter been killed, known as he was to favor Hitler? And what had he been doing in Egypt?

Who was the man who had been shot aboard the *Semiramis*? Where had he obtained the scarab ring? Why did he want to talk to Ponga Jim and no one else? And what was his connection with the girl, Zara Hammedan?

And last but not least, what could Ponga Jim Mayo possibly know that the enemy might fear?

Whatever it was, it had to be something he had known before he left Africa, several years before. There seemed only one answer to that. He would have to go over all his African experience in his mind, recalling each fact, each incident, each person. Somewhere he would find a clue.

In the meanwhile, he would have to avoid the police, and

even more, the killers who would be sure to be on his trail. The card that had been found on the dead man, the card bearing the name of Zara Hammedan, was the only good lead Ponga Jim had, and to Zara Hammedan he would go.

He had already learned that she lived in the Ramleh section of Alexandria. So at eight o'clock, moving up through the trees, Ponga Jim looked up at the Moorish palace that was Zara Hammedan's home. There were no windows on the lower floor; just a high, blank wall of stucco. Above that, the second floor projected over the narrow alley on either side of the house, and there were many windows, all brilliantly lighted.

A limousine rolled up to the entrance, and two men in evening dress got out. For an instant the light touched the face of one of them. He was Nathan Demarest!

As other cars began to arrive, Ponga Jim studied the house thoughtfully. Had there been no crowd he would have shed his disguise, approached the house, and sent his own name to the lady. But now—

Keeping under the cypress trees, he worked down along the alley. At one place the branches of a huge tree reached out toward the window opposite it. Ponga Jim caught a branch and swung himself into the tree with the agility of a monkey. Creeping out along the branch, he glanced through the window into a bedroom, obviously a woman's room. At the moment, it was empty.

The window was barred, and the heavy bars were welded together and set into steel slides in the window casing. Ponga Jim crept farther along the branch, a big one that had been cut off when it touched the house. Balancing himself, he tested the bars. Almost noiselessly, they lifted when he strained.

They wouldn't weigh a bit under eighty pounds, and it was an awkward lift, even though he had often put up more than twice that with one hand. Looking about, he found a fair-sized branch and cut it off with his seaman's clasp knife. Then, leaning far out, he worked the set of bars up and propped the stick beneath them.

*   *   *

It was quite dark, and in the dim light Ponga Jim could see nothing beneath him. Once, he thought he detected a movement, but when he waited, there was no more movement, no sound. He pushed the window open with his foot and slipped through the window.

Below, in the darkness, the jungle-keen ears of Big London, who had been watching Ponga Jim slowly working the bars up, had heard a soft step. He faded into the brush as softly as a big cat. A man slid slowly from the dark and glanced around, trying to place the black man, and then slid a knife from his sleeve. And as Ponga Jim leaned far out toward the window, he drew the knife back to throw.

A huge black hand closed around his throat, and he was fairly jerked from his feet. Struggling, he tried to use the knife, but it was plucked from his nerveless fingers by the big black. Before the man knew what was happening, he was neatly trussed hand and foot and then gagged. Dimly, he saw a huge form bending above him, making a threatening motion with the knife. Frightened, the would-be killer was silent.

Ponga Jim gently closed the window behind him and glanced around. There was a faint perfume in the room. He crossed to the dressing table and slid open a drawer. Inside were some letters. He had started to glance over them when a voice in the hall startled him. Instantly, he dropped the packet into the drawer and stepped quickly across the room and into a closet.

The door opened and a woman came in. Or rather a girl, followed by a maid. Her hair was black, and her eyes were long, large, and slightly oblique. Her white evening gown fitted her like a dream and revealed rather than concealed her slender, curved figure.

She wore a simple jade necklace that Ponga Jim could see was very old. Standing in the darkness, he watched through the crack of the closet door, fearful that the maid might come to the closet.

Zara Hammedan, for it was obviously she, glanced up once, straight at the door behind which he stood. Then the maid started across the room toward him.

"No, Miriam," Zara said suddenly, "just leave the things. I'll take care of them. You may go now. If anyone asks for me, tell them I'll be down shortly."

The maid stepped from the room and drew the door closed. Zara touched her hair lightly and then put her hand in a drawer and lifted a small, but businesslike automatic. Then she looked at the closet door.

"You may come out now," she said evenly, "but be careful! You should clean the sand from your shoes."

Ponga Jim Mayo pushed the door open and stepped out, closing it behind him.

"You," he said smiling, "are a smart girl."

"Who are you?" she demanded. Her face showed no emotion, but he was struck again by its vivid beauty.

"I am a man who found another man murdered in his cabin," Ponga Jim said quietly, "and that man had your name written on a card that was in his pocket. So I came to you."

"You choose an odd way of presenting yourself," Zara said. "Who was this man?"

"I do not know," Jim said. "He came to see me, and in his pocket was a ring with an emerald scarab."

She caught her breath.

"When did this happen?"

"Shortly after midnight. The man was shot by someone using a silencer from across the street. So far the police know nothing about the murder. Or about the ring or your name."

"Why did I not know of this?" she asked. "It seems—"

"One of your present guests knows," Ponga Jim said. "Nathan Demarest."

"He?" She stared at him wide-eyed. "But who are you?"

He smiled. "I'm Ponga Jim Mayo," he said.

"Oh!" She rose. "I have heard of you. You came here, then, to learn about the murdered man?"

"Partly." He sat down and took off the headcloth. "The rest is to find what he wanted to tell me, where he got that ring, and what you know about a certain warship now in the Red Sea. Also, what there is to this Moslem movement you're heading."

She smiled at him. "What makes you think all of these questions have anything to do with me?"

"I know they have," he said. "And I've got to know the answers, because somebody's trying to kill me. I was attacked last night, shoved in the harbor by a killer."

"You?" she exclaimed. "Was it a man with a scar across his nose?"

"Sure," Ponga Jim said. "That's him." He took a cigarette from a sandalwood box and lit it. Then he handed it to her. "A friend of yours?"

"No!" The loathing in her voice was plain. "But the man was a pearl diver from Kuwait. I don't see how—"

"How I got away? I've done some diving myself, lady, and a lot of fighting. Now give. What's this all about?"

"I can't tell you," Zara said. "Only—if you want to live, take your ship and leave Egypt, and don't ever come back!"

"That's not hospitality," he said, grinning, "especially from a beautiful girl. No, I'm not leaving. I've been warned before and threatened before. I've as healthy a respect for my own hide as the next man, but never have found you could dodge trouble by running. My way is to meet it halfway. Now somebody wants my hide. I'd like to see the guy. I'd like to see what he wants and if he knows how to get it."

"He does. And I'll tell you nothing but this—the dead man was Rudolf Burne, and you are marked for death because of three things. You beat a man playing poker once who never was beaten before or since, you know where the emerald ring came from, and you know where the warship is!"

"*I* do?" Ponga Jim stared. "But—"

"You'll have to go now!" Zara said suddenly, her eyes wide. "Quick! There's someone coming!"

He hurried to the window. She stood behind him, biting her lip. Suddenly he realized she was trembling with fear.

"Go!" she insisted. "Quickly!"

"Sure." He slid open the window and put a leg over the sill. "But never let it be said that Jim Mayo failed to say good-bye." Slipping one arm around Zara's waist, he kissed her before she could draw back. "Goodnight," said Ponga Jim. "I'll be seeing you!"

As the steel grate slid into place, he heard the door open. Then he was back in the foliage of the tree and in a matter of seconds had slid to the ground.

"Now," he told himself, "I'll—"

At a movement behind him he whirled, but something crashed down on his head with stunning force. There was an instant of blinding pain when he struggled to fight back the wave of darkness sweeping over him, then another blow, and he plunged forward into a limitless void.

CHAPTER V
In a Tomb

When Ponga Jim's eyes opened he was lying on his back in almost total darkness. A thin ray of light from a crack overhead tried feebly to penetrate the gloom. He tried to sit up, only to find he was bound hand and foot and very securely.

His head throbbed with agony, and the tightly bound ropes made his hands numb. After an instant of futile effort, he lay still, letting his eyes rove the darkness. The place had rock walls, he could see—one wall at least. There seemed to be some kind of inscriptions or paintings on the wall, but he couldn't make them out.

The air was dry, and when he stirred a powdery dust lifted from the floor.

Lying in the darkness he tried to assemble his thoughts. Most of all there hammered at his brain the insistent reminder that he, himself, knew the answers to the puzzling questions that had brought him to this situation. Zara had told him that he knew the man behind the scenes, where the ship was, and where the ring had come from.

But there was something else—a memory he couldn't place, a sensation of lying in the bottom of a boat and hearing voices. Now he slowly pieced together that memory, scowling with effort to force the thought back to consciousness. In that swaying darkness he half remembered, with spray on his face and damp boards against his back, he seemed to have heard a guttural voice saying in triumph:

"That will be the biggest convoy of all! Forty ships, and they are helpless before the *Khamsin*."

Then another voice that had muttered, "And only two days to wait!"

Ponga Jim Mayo lay still, his head throbbing. For the first time in a life of fierce brawls, barroom brannigans, gunfights, and war on land and sea, he was helpless. Not only was he imprisoned somewhere far from civilization, he was sure, but he was bound so tightly that even to wriggle seemed impossible. The feeling came over him that he was not just imprisoned. He had been carried here to die.

His mind sorted out his memories. The warship was in the Red Sea. Zara had told him that something in his own past, something he had forgotten but another remembered, linked him with the base of the warship.

Carefully, trying to neglect nothing, he tried to recall that long, narrow, reef-strewn sea of milky, sickly water. He remembered the sandstorms sweeping across the sea from the desert, the days of endless calm and impossible heat when the thermometer soared past one hundred and thirty degrees.

He remembered rocky islets and endless, jagged coral teeth

ready to tear the bottom from a ship, sandy shores where desert tribesmen lurked, ready to raid and pillage any helpless ship, pirates now as they had been ages ago in Solomon's time.

And along those mountainous, volcanic shores where no rain fell were ruins—ruins of the heyday of Mohammed, of Solomon, of Pharaohs; ruins whose names and origins were lost in the mists of antiquity. No like area in all the world has so many ruined cities as the shores of the Red Sea and the edge of Arabia where it faces the Indian Ocean.

Even in Mokha, once the center of the coffee trade, in 1824 a city of twenty thousand inhabitants with a shifting population that made it much larger, only two or three hundred Somalis, Arabs, and Jews now lived in ruined houses of stone, crawling like animals in rags from their lairs, cowardly and abject, but ready to fight like demons if need be. Mokha was now only a memory, with its streets heaped with debris, its stone piers crumbling into the stagnant, soupy sea.

Yet somewhere along the shores of the Red Sea was a base. A base that must be well equipped and fitted for at least minor repairs, with tanks filled with water and fuel oil. But where?

His memory searched around Hanish Island, around many a Ghubbet and khor, down the Masira Channel and past Ras Markaz, across the dreaded Rakka shoals and up to Jiddah town, where the Tomb of Eve with its wide, white dome stands among the old windmills.

Somewhere in that heat, sand, and desolate emptiness was the base for the battleship of mystery he had seen.

Now Europe, Asia, and even America were at war, and in the Near East the bazaars were rife with whispers of intrigue, with stories of impending rebellion, of the gathering desert tribes, of restlessness along the Tihama, of gatherings in the Druse hills. And then out of the night—murder.

Hard-bitten old General McKnight, who knew the East as few men did—murdered, poisoned with his own sherry. And Norfolk, shrewd criminal investigator, stabbed suddenly on a dark street. One by one the men who could fight this new evil, this strange, growing power, one by one they were dying, murdered by unseen hands at the direction of a man who sat far behind the scenes pulling the strings upon which puppets moved to kill.

Ponga Jim stirred restlessly. That was the horror of it, to know that he knew the clue, that somewhere down the chaotic background of his past was the knowledge that could end all this killing here.

Suddenly, he stiffened. There had been a movement, a sly, slithering sound. And for the first time, he became conscious of a peculiar odor in the place. His eyes had gradually grown accustomed to the dim light, and now, with a skin-crawling horror, he saw!

On a heap of broken stone and piled earthen jars was a huge snake, lifting its ugly flat head and looking toward him! His throat constricting with terror, Ponga Jim's eyes roved again. And now that he could distinguish things better and in the dim vagueness could see grotesque figures of carts, animals, and workmen painted on the walls, he knew he was in a tomb! He was lying where a sarcophagus once had lain, on a stone table probably three or four feet above the floor.

Turning his head, he could see the dim outlines of great coils, more snakes. And still more.

He looked up, cold sweat breaking out on his forehead, and it dawned upon him what had been done. Above, a loosely fitted stone slab had been moved back, and his body had been lowered into this old tomb. Soon he would fall off the table to the floor, and the snakes would bite. Or he would die of thirst or of starvation.

Ponga Jim felt with his feet toward the edge of the stone table. He got his ankles over, and a thrill went through him as what he had hoped proved true. The edge of the stone slab on which he lay was clean-cut, sharp!

Hooking his ankles over the edge, he began to saw. It would take a long time, but it would have to be. A snake moved, rearing its head to stare, but he worked on as sweat soaked his clothing.

It seemed that hours passed, but still he worked, on and on. Above him, the light grew dim and darkness closed down.

Suddenly, dust spilled in his face, and above him he heard a grating as of stone on stone. He looked up, and above him was a square of sky and stars, blotted out suddenly by an enormous shape.

"Captain Jim?" The voice was husky with effort. "You down there, Captain?"

"You're right I am!" Ponga Jim's voice was hoarse with relief. "Watch it! I'm tied hand and foot, and this place is crawling with snakes. Get a line and rig a hook on it."

"Captain, they ain't no more line up here than there's nothin'! This here place is nothing but rock and sand. Ain't no fit place for no snake even."

"Wait!"

In desperation, Ponga Jim hacked viciously at the edge of the slab and suddenly felt the weakened strands give. He hacked again, kicking downward against the stone edge, sawing, jerking against the corner.

The snakes were stirring restlessly now. He knew what would happen if one struck him. Within an instant he would be bitten a hundred times. Snakes, like rats and men, can be gang fighters.

But the rope fell loose.

He crawled to his feet, staggered, and almost toppled from the table into the crawling mass below.

Ponga Jim's hands were bound, but even if they had not been it was a good ten feet to the hole above.

"London," he called, "scout around and find something to haul me out of here or I'll start knotting these snakes together. If I do I swear I'll toss you the hot end to hold!"

"Don't you be doing that!" Big London said hastily. "I'll see what I can find."

Ponga Jim bent over, working his slender hips between the circle of his arms and bound wrists. Once he had them down over his hips he stepped back through the circle and straightened up, his arms in front of him. Then he began working at the knot with his teeth. It was a matter of minutes until the knots were untied.

Shaking the ropes loose, he gathered up the pieces. He had about eight feet of rope; a bit less when he had knotted the two together with a sheet bend.

There was sound above him.

"Captain"—Big London's voice was worried—"I reckon you going to have to start working on them snakes. They ain't nothing up here like no rope."

"Lie down!" Ponga Jim said, "and catch this rope! I'll toss it up, you take a good hold, and then I'm climbing. And you better not let go!"

"You just leave it to London, Captain," the black man assured him. "I'll not let go!"

Big London caught the rope deftly. Then Ponga Jim went up, hand over hand. When he reached Big London's hands, he grabbed the big man's wrist. London let go of the rope and caught him. In a few seconds he was standing in the open air.

"Thanks, pal!" Ponga Jim said fervently. "I've been in some spots, but that one—"

"Captain," Big London said, "we better be going. This is clean across the Gulf of Suez and way down the coast. They spent the best part of the night and morning coming down here."

Ponga Jim looked around. It was bright moonlight.

"Is there a high cliff right over there?" He pointed toward the southeast. "One that drops off into the water? And is there a black hill right over there?"

"Sure is, Captain," Big London said. "I took me that black hill for a landmark. I smuggled myself away on their boat, hoping they'd leave one man alone so I could take over, but they never. Then I waited hid out till they took you ashore. I wanted to follow, but they got clean away with three men with guns still on the boat. I had to slip over into the water when they started again, swim ashore, and then trail you up here."

"You did a good job." Ponga Jim chuckled. "The joke is on them. This place is the Ras Muhammed, the tip of Sinai Peninsula, and right over there, not three miles from here, in one of the neatest little bays in this area, is the *Semiramis!*"

An hour and a little more passed before they reached the shore of the little inlet surrounded by high cliffs. At a cleft in the rock they made their way down to a beach of black sand and decomposed coral. The freighter was anchored, a dark blotch, not a hundred yards offshore. At Ponga Jim's shout, a boat was hastily lowered.

No sooner had Ponga Jim reached the freighter than he called Brophy.

"Slug," he said, "get number five open and break out that amphibian. I want her tuned and ready to take off by daybreak. This is going to be quick work."

He walked into the cabin, tossed off his clothes, and fell into his bunk. In seconds he was sound asleep.

CHAPTER VI
Mystery Leader

Four men and a woman sat in the spacious living room of Zara Hammedan's Ramleh residence. Zara's face was composed, and only her eyes showed a hint of the strain she was undergoing.

One of the men stood up. He was well over six feet and broad shouldered, and he moved ·with the ease of a big cat. There was a great deal of the cat about him—in his eyes, in the movements of his hands. His hair was black, but white at the temples, and his eyes were large and intensely black. His face was swarthy and his arched eyebrows heavy. There was about

172

him something that spoke of a sense of power, of command, and in every word, every gesture, was an utter ruthlessness.

"You see, gentlemen?" he said lightly. "Our plans move swiftly. There was a momentary danger, but Captain Mayo has been taken care of. He was dropped into the Tomb of the Snakes this morning. By this time he has been dead for hours. By tomorrow noon the convoy will be well into the Red Sea. It carries fifty thousand soldiers, many planes, much petrol, and much ammunition. By tomorrow at dark that convoy will be completely destroyed. As always, there will be no survivors.

"And tomorrow night? General Kernan and Major Arnold will be shot down. Within an hour a reign of terror will begin in Cairo, Alexandria, Port Said, Suez, Beirut, Damascus, Baghdad, and Aleppo. By tomorrow night at midnight, the British will be leaderless in the Near East. Rebellion will break out." The man paused. "Then we will take over."

"I do not like it." The man who spoke was slender and bald, and his small eyes were shrewd. "It is not practical. And that Ponga Jim was disposed of in too theatrical a manner. He should have been shot. I would never leave such a man alive."

"The man is just a man." The imperious words of the tall man were smooth, cold. "One would think, Herr Heittn, that you thought him supernatural."

Heittn smiled thinly. "I know this man," he said shortly. "Did I not use every means to dispose of him? Did he not kill my brother? Did he not handle Count Kull like he was a child?"

"Strength is not enough," the tall man said. "It takes brains!"

"You got something there, Chief," one of the other men said. His jaw was heavy, his nose flat. He looked like a good heavyweight boxer. "But I been hearing about this guy Mayo. He's a tough cookie."

"But I know how to handle 'tough cookies,' Mullens," the tall man assured. "You have only to handle your end. You have your men ready?"

"You bet," Mullens said. "I got four of the best rodmen that

173

ever slung a heater. All of 'em with tommy guns. We'll mow your pals Kernan and Arnold down like they were dummies."

"Then we're all ready. You're sure about the time, Demarest?"

"Yes," said Demarest. "The time is right. Everything will move perfectly. The destruction of this convoy, the fourth consecutive convoy to be totally destroyed, will wreck the troops' morale. A whispering campaign has begun. Kernan cannot be replaced. He knows the East too well."

Heittn was watching the tall man steadily, his eyes curious.

"I don't understand your stake in this, Theron," he said abruptly. "What is it you want? You are not German. You are not just an adventurer. I do not understand."

"No reason why you should, Herr Heittn," the man called Theron snapped. "You have a task to do. You will do it. What you think or do not think is of no interest to me if your task is well done."

Zara arose and excused herself. Theron's eyes followed her as she left the room. They were cold, curious.

"What of her?" Demarest asked. "You are sure of her?"

"I will be responsible for her, Demarest. She has too much power among the Arabs not to be of value to us. But she must be kept with us always."

The group broke up. Heittn was first to leave. He took his hat and started for the door, then glanced swiftly around, and with surprising speed darted up the stairs toward Zara's room. There he tapped lightly on the door.

It opened at once, and before Zara could speak, Heittn slipped into the room. He looked at the girl narrowly.

"What do you want?" she demanded.

The German looked down at the small automatic in her hand.

"You will not need that, Fräulein," he said gently. "What I want is of interest to us both. I want to know about *him*." He pointed downward. "Can we trust him? What does he want? Who is he?"

Zara's face paled. She glanced toward the door. It was locked. She crossed to the window, started to close it, and then caught her breath. The steel bars were gone!

But when she turned, her face was composed.

"I know no more than you, Herr Heittn," she said calmly, "except he seems to have unlimited funds. Also, he is ambitious."

Heittn nodded. "Ah!" he said seriously. "That is what I have seen, Fräulein. He is ambitious. Too ambitious. And he has power, too much power. Sometimes"—he shook his head worriedly—"I think he is beyond us all, that man. He is not a Nazi, yet he is too strong with the party for me, who am a Nazi."

"But what could he do?" Zara protested.

"Do? A strong man with money, ambition, and courage—what can he not do in such times as these? Nations are rising and falling; men are discouraged, afraid. They will look everywhere for shelter. The weak admire the strong, and that one, he is strong. He is cruel. I admit it, Fräulein. I am afraid of him!"

Casually Zara Hammedan lighted a cigarette. Her eyes strayed toward the closet door, now closed. She frowned a little. The bars from the window had been slid up out of sight again, and that could mean but one thing. Ponga Jim Mayo was somewhere in the house.

She looked at the German shrewdly. "Herr Heittn, your government does not appeal to me, you know that. But I would even prefer the dictatorship of Nazi Germany to what would follow the success of these schemes in the Near East! I do not know more about that man than you do, but I do know that Captain Mayo knew, or knows, something that he does not wish anyone to know."

"And Mayo is dead," Heittn said slowly.

"Perhaps." Zara flicked the ash from her cigarette. "You had better go, Herr Heittn. It grows late."

The Nazi turned to the door and then glanced around.

"I go, but I have a plan to make our friend below be a bit

175

more reasonable. He has been too ambitious. But there are ways— " He smiled. *"Guten Abend, Fräulein!"*

As Heittn walked swiftly down the hall he glanced over the stairs, but no one was in sight. With a quick smile, Heittn went down the carpeted stairs. He had reached the door when a voice froze him in his tracks. Something in the low, even tone sent a chill up his spine. He turned slowly.

Theron stood in the shadow near the door from the wide living room. The light fell across his face. There was something regal in his appearance. In his right hand, he held a German Luger.

"I thought you left us, Herr Heittn?" he said coldly. "I do not like spies!"

"Spies?" Heittn shrugged. "Come, come, Theron! That is hardly the term. I went up to see Miss Hammedan about—"

"But searched my room in the meantime, is that it? Give me that blueprint, Herr Heittn. Give it to me, at once!"

"Blueprint?" The Nazi was puzzled. "I don't understand."

Above in the darkness, Zara slipped from her room and looked down. In her hand was an automatic. She hesitated and then lifted it slowly.

"Don't!"

A hand closed over her wrist, and the voice that spoke to her was low. Demarest stepped up beside her.

"Not now," he said. "Without him, nothing would work. He holds all the strings. The whole plot would be useless and we would be exposed."

In the silence they could hear the words that were being spoken at the front door.

"All right, Herr Heittn," Theron was saying. "It does not matter. But if the blueprint were to leave this house, it would matter. None can enter or leave, however, unless I know. You have hidden it here or have it on you. I do not need it—or you!"

The sound of the automatic was flat and ugly in the dim hallway. Heittn's face went sick, and the man stepped back, two short steps. Then he sat down, abruptly, with a thin trickle of blood coming from the hole over his heart.

Her face deathly pale, Zara Hammedan turned abruptly and went to her room. Nathan Demarest glanced after her and then shrugged and returned to his own room.

Zara closed the door and then turned. In the dim light the man sitting on the bed was plainly visible. His peaked cap lay on the bed beside him, and he still wore the faded khaki suit and woven-leather sandals. She could see the butt of his automatic under the edge of his coat.

"You—you must go quickly!" she protested. "He killed Herr Heittn. He will stop at nothing now!"

"Heittn here?" Ponga Jim lifted an eyebrow. "What I want to know is—who's he?"

"I mean Theron," she whispered. "He will be coming up, too, wanting to know what Heittn said to me. Go—quickly!"

Ponga Jim's eyes were bright.

"Theron! Why didn't I—?" He stepped to the window, put a foot over the sill, and reached for the thick branch. "So long, beautiful. Be seeing you!"

CHAPTER VII
Ponga Jim Takes a Chance

Ponga Jim had reached the ground and was starting to slip back into the trees when he saw them. Four men closing in on him.

He knew what that meant, and he didn't hesitate. He jumped the nearest one, hooking a left short and hard to the man's head. It hit with a *plop*, and the man's head flew back. He dropped like a sack of meal.

A shot clipped by his head, and Ponga Jim dropped into a

crouch as his own gun came out. The big automatic roared. Once—twice—three times.

Two men dropped, a third screamed shrilly and staggered back into the building. Holding his left shoulder, Ponga Jim ran. He dodged through the trees with bullets clipping the leaves about him, ducked into an alley, and then crossed into another street. A car was waiting with the motor running. He jumped in.

"Move!" he said, and Sakim let the car into gear and stepped on the gas.

Ponga Jim glanced at his watch. It was three A.M. At noon the convoy would be attacked, and he had until then, and until then only. It was going to be nip and tuck if he made it.

He felt sick. Fifty thousand soldiers coming up the Red Sea toward Suez, fifty thousand Anzacs to strengthen the Army of the Nile. He knew the plot now. What he had overheard and what he had found in his ransacking of Theron's room had told him the whole story.

Native mobs running riot in the streets, men dying by the thousand—Kernan, Arnold, all of them.

The car slowed up as it neared the American Export Line's office on the Rue Fouad. A man stepped from the shadows, and the car whined to a halt. Major Arnold hit the running board with a jump.

"Jim! What's happened?" Arnold's face was tense. "When Selim found me he said all calamity was to break loose today. What do you know?"

As the car raced across town, Ponga Jim told his story quickly and concisely.

"Ptolemais Theron is the man behind it all," he said. "He's a bad one, William! I've known of him for years. He and I played poker once with two other men in the place of Mahr-el-din in the Kasbah. Ring Wallace was there and Ski Jorgenson. Theron had just sidestepped a term on the breakwater for illicit diamond buying and was working on a deal to sell a lot of world war rifles to the Riffs. We were talking of the Red Sea, and Ski—"

Ponga Jim stopped short, and his face went blank.

"By heaven, William, I've got it!"

"Got what?" Arnold's face was tight, stiff.

"William"—Ponga Jim's voice was low with emotion—"Ski Jorgenson had been working a salvage job in the Gulf of Aqaba, near Tirān Island. He told us of finding some huge caverns under the cliffs of the islands—one room five hundred yards long, with a dozen chambers opening off from it, and water in that main chamber. He told us about what a swell smuggler's hangout it would be. And the entrance is deep. A ship could come and go—if it had no masts!"

"You mean that's the base of that mystery battlewagon?" Arnold's face lit up. "By the Lord Harry, if it is we'll blast the place in on them!"

"That's the base. Theron wanted me killed because I knew too much. When Ski told about the caverns he also told some stuff about the ancient tombs at Adulis, and the chances are Theron's been robbing them for the gold to put this deal over. That would be where Rudolf Burne got the emerald ring he had. Probably he was in on the deal, got cold feet, and came to me because he knew I wouldn't turn him over to the police. But he was shot before he could talk."

The car slid to a halt, and Arnold dropped out.

"Don't worry about us," he said drily. "We'll be all set."

"Wait!" Ponga Jim put a hand on Arnold's arm. "Don't say a thing about yourselves—I mean you and General Kernan. I've already arranged for that. I'm going to have Selim, Sakim, Big London, and Longboy standing by. They'll get the men who'll be sent to kill you.

"Don't trust anyone. Somebody high up is in this, somebody close to you." He paused. "Oh, yes! Remember Carter? He built the *Khamsin*. Built the plant for it for the Nazis."

"Okay." Arnold smiled suddenly and held out his hand. "I don't know what you've got up your sleeve, but good luck. And in case something slips up—it's been a grand fight!"

Ponga Jim grinned. "Listen, pal. Just to keep the record straight. Keep Zara Hammedan under cover. She means well, and— "

"Who?" William grabbed Ponga Jim's arm. "Why, you didn't mention her! Where did you—"

"Shh!" Mayo said, grinning. "It's late, William, and you'll wake up the neighbors. Zara? Oh, we're just like that!" He held up two fingers. "A honey, isn't she?"

Selim stepped on the gas.

"I hope you get shot!" Arnold yelled after him.

Tirān Island, at the southern end of the Gulf of Aqaba, is six and a half miles long and in the south part is about five miles wide. Chisholm Point is steep and cliffy, but Johnson Point, the northwest tip of the island, is low and flat, of sand and dead coral. South of the point, two flat, sandy beaches afford good landing, but the coast elsewhere consists of undercut coral cliffs.

It lacked but a little of daylight when Ponga Jim Mayo stepped ashore on one of those sandy beaches. Slug Brophy scowled at him in the vague light.

"I don't like it, Skipper. I don't like shooting at no ship when you're aboard it. And if they catch you they'll fill you so full of lead you'll sink clean through to China."

"Forget it," said Mayo. "I've got my job to do—you've got yours. Have the boats and life rafts ready, see? We've got one chance in a million that the *Semiramis* will come out of this, but a chance. All I'm figuring on is crippling the *Khamsin*— that's the name of the mystery battleship—so she can't move fast. Then maybe she can be kept busy until the convoy escapes. Have the sub over right away. Jeff and Hifty from the engine room can handle it."

The boat shoved off into the darkness, and Ponga Jim climbed the gradually shelving beach. He paused there, looking over the island: sand, decomposed coral, and rock, with here and there some grass. He was going on a memory of what Ski Jorgenson had said several years before, that there was an opening of the cave to the island itself, aside from the huge mouth that opened into the gulf.

He found it by sheer good luck, after he had looked for an hour. It was already daylight when he saw the small hole Ski had mentioned. Surprisingly, there was no one near it. He slid through and found himself in a passage where he could stand erect. He hurried, hesitated at a branching passage, and then chose the larger. It opened into the huge cavern so suddenly that he almost walked right out into the open.

Even so, he stopped in his tracks, staring. He stood in the darkness at one side of a huge cavern, its domed roof lost in the shadows overhead. But what held his gaze was the warship.

It was at least five hundred feet long, painted black, but glistening with metallic luster. The hull seemed to be built like that of any battleship, but above deck the ship was covered with a turtleshell covering. There were two turrets forward and one aft, each looking much like slightly less than half a ball where the rounded surface lifted above the shell. The turrets, obviously, could turn to cover any point from dead ahead to a complete right angle on either side.

Between, in three tiers, like guns in a fort, were smaller guns. Nowhere on the ship was there any exposed deck, any open space. The ship was completely covered with a steel housing from stem to stern.

There were lights around the ship, and men working. Ponga Jim could hear the clangor of metal and could see a great moving crane, and obviously the branch caverns were fitted with shops for the building and upkeep of ships.

Keeping in the shadows, Ponga Jim worked his way to a place where the cavern narrowed. His plan was to get aboard and keep the quarter pint of nitroglycerine he had intact— which meant keeping himself intact.

Dozens of men were working and sweating. Armed guards patrolled the area near the ship, and at any moment Ponga Jim

181

knew he might be seen. Warily, he dodged behind a pile of oil drums, waiting.

The German who came around the corner of the pile came without any warning, and Ponga Jim looked up to see the man staring at him. He saw the man's eyes widen, saw his mouth open, and then Ponga Jim took a chance and smashed a right hand into the man's belly. If the fellow knocked him down with that nitro in his pocket—

The big German's breath was knocked out of him, but he swung a wicked punch while trying to yell. And somehow he got out a knife. Mayo ducked the punch, and smashed both hands into the man's wind, but then the knife came down in a vicious stabbing cut. Ponga Jim started to duck, but the knife struck him, and he felt the blade bury itself in his side. He grabbed the man's wrist and tore his hand loose. Then he smashed his fist into the German's throat, smashed and smashed again.

Fiercely, in darkness and silence, their breath coming in great gasps, the two fought. A terrific punch rocked Ponga Jim's head, and that smoky taste when rocked by a bad one came into his mouth. Then he smashed another punch to the Nazi's windpipe and hit him hard across the Adam's apple with the edge of his hand. The German went down, and Ponga Jim bent over him, slugging him again.

There was no choice. Even now if the man were found, they would search and Ponga Jim would die. And not only he would die, but fifty thousand soldiers would die, men would die in Alexandria, Cairo, and Port Said; for the news of the attacked convoy was to be the signal for the beginning of the slaughter. Innocent people would die and brave men. Worse, a tyrant as evil as Hitler would come to power here in the Near East, a killer as ruthless as a shark of the sea, as remorseless as a slinking tiger.

The Nazi sank at Ponga Jim's feet. Behind the piled drums as they were, they had remained unseen. He picked the big German up and felt a white-hot streak of agony along his side.

Remembering a huge crack in the cavern floor back about fifty feet, he carried the man over to it and dropped him in. He did not hear the body strike bottom.

"Sorry, pal," he muttered, "but this is war. It was you or them."

Creeping back, he studied the ship. There was no activity in front of him. That meant a chance. He walked out of the shadow and calmly went up the gangway into the ship. A man glanced up, but at the distance Ponga Jim must have looked like any other officer, for the man went on with his work.

Ponga Jim found himself in an electrically lighted tunnel. He could see the amazingly thick steel of the ship's hull as he went forward, walking fast. He passed several doors until he got well forward. Then he went into a storeroom.

He found a place secure from observation, slipped off his coat, and, taking a deep breath, drew the knife from the wound. It had gone into the muscle back of his ribs from front to back. He plugged the wound and then relaxed.

CHAPTER VIII
The Convoy Is Safe

It was the throb of engines that awakened Ponga Jim. Dimly he was conscious they had been going for some time. By the feel of the ship he knew they were in open water.

Timing was important. The convoy's attempted destruction would begin it. Ponga Jim rolled back the sacks and stepped out into the storeroom. He glanced at his wristwatch. It was early yet.

He went to the port and glanced out. The sea was calm, only white around the coral. The sun was hot and the air clear except for the dancing heat waves over the rocky shore.

He looked again, and his hands gripped the rim of the port.

He felt his heart give a great leap. They were nearing Gordon Reef in the Strait of Tirān! He saw the small, iron ship plainly visible on the rocks of the reef; the wreck had been there so long it was hardly noticed anymore.

But today it meant more. Today, if all went well, a pocket submarine of a hundred tons would be lying there, waiting— the submarine he had captured in the Well of the Unholy Light, on Halmahera.

He was watching, yet even then he could just barely see the ripple of foam when the sub's periscope lifted. In his ears he could hear words as though he were there himself. He could hear Jeff speaking to his one-man crew: "Fire one!" Then, after a few seconds, "Fire two!"

Ponga Jim saw the white streak of a torpedo and heard someone sing out above; then he saw the second streak. The big warship was jarred with a terrific explosion and then a second or two later, with a second. A shell crashed in the water only dozens of feet from the tiny sub. But the periscope was gone now.

Ponga Jim gripped his hands until the fingernails bit into his palms. How much damage had been done? Would Jeff and Hifty get away? Thank God the warship had no destroyer screen to pursue and drop depth bombs.

There was shouting forward, and he could feel the ship slowing down. He set his jaw. Now it was up to him. Now he would do what he came for and end this scourge of the sea once and for all.

He found a uniform in the pile of junk in the storeroom and crawled into it. Then he stepped out into the passage again.

No one seemed to notice him. Men were running and shouting in the steel tunnel. He joined those hurrying men. He gathered that the first torpedo had hit right where he had wanted it to. From the stolen blueprint, which covered a section of the bow, he had known that the extreme bow and stern of the warship were but thinly armored. Elsewhere, twenty inches of steel protected the waterline. The second fish had wasted itself against that steel bulwark.

As he dashed forward, a man passed him, and Ponga Jim saw a startled look come into the man's face. The fellow stopped, and Ponga Jim ducked into the passage leading down. A moment later he heard a man yelling, and swore viciously. To be discovered now!

At a breakneck pace he went down the steel ladder. Water was pouring in through the side into one of the blisters below. Into two of them. He heard a petty officer assuring another that the damage was localized, that the *Khamsin* would be slowed a little, but was in no danger of sinking.

Above them, Ponga Jim heard a shouted order. He ducked toward a steel door in the bulkhead. The petty officer shouted at him in German, but he plunged through. Then he stopped and placed the bottle of nitrogylcerine against the steel bulkhead.

The door swung open again, and Ponga Jim flattened against the bulkhead. Men dashed through. On impulse, Ponga Jim stooped, caught up the bottle and sprang back through the door and then ran for the ladder. A man shouted and grabbed at him, but he swung viciously and knocked the man sprawling into a corner. Another man leaped at him with a spanner, and Ponga Jim scrambled up the ladder and then wheeled and hurled the bottle into the corner near the damaged side of the ship!

There was a terrific blast of white flame, shot through with crimson. Ponga Jim felt himself seized as though by a giant hand and hurled against the wall. He went down with a jangle of bells in his head, and above him he could hear the roar of guns, the sound of shells bursting, and a fearful roaring in his head. . . .

Ponga Jim fought back to consciousness to find himself lying on some burst sacks. Struggling to get to his knees, he realized the deck was canted forward.

There was blood all over him. He turned, and sickened at the sight that met his eyes. The deck was covered with blood, and a half dozen men lay around him, their bodies torn and bloody. He crawled to the wall, pulled himself up, and glanced down into the yawning chasm where he had thrown the nitro.

The compartment was full of water, and it was still rising, slowly but surely. He started aft, feeling his way along the steel tunnel in the dark.

His head throbbed, and something was wrong with one of his legs. He had an awful feeling that part of it was gone, but he struggled along, conscious of a steady burning in his side.

The world was full of thunder, and he could hear the heavy crash of the mighty eighteen-inch guns above him. He was thankful he had stuffed his ears with cotton before starting this. He had known there would be a battle. But were they shelling the convoy? He fought his way to a port and, wiping the blood from his eyes, stared out.

In a kind of madness he saw, across the world of smoke and flame, the ugly stern of the old *Semiramis*. Her rusty sides were scarred with red lead, but the three 5.9s that were aft were firing steadily.

With a stretch of coral reef between the *Semiramis* and the warship, and the freighter itself almost out of sight in the deep, high-walled inlet where it had been concealed, she presented a small target and one that called for careful firing. It was too close for the big guns and in an awkward position for the smaller guns. Gunner Millan, he saw, was doing just what he had been told to do. All three of the 5.9s were aimed at one spot on the bow of the *Khamsin* and were pounding away remorselessly.

But the *Khamsin* was not staying to fight. The convoy was still to be attacked, and crippled though the mystery battle-wagon was, she had only to get out into the sea to bring those big eighteen-inch guns to bear on that convoy. She was injured, but proceeding as scheduled.

Clinging to the port, Ponga Jim heard an ominous roaring. Then he saw a V-shaped formation of bombing planes. The first one dipped and then another, and then the warship was roaring with exploding bombs. He turned from the port and started aft again.

Dazed, he staggered from side to side of the tunnel. He had done what he could. What remained was for the navy to do. He staggered forward, saw a steel door in the hull, and fell to his knees, clawing at the dogs. He got one loose and then another.

Suddenly there was a wild shout. A man was rushing toward him, his face twisted with fury. Nathan Demarest! He sprang at Ponga Jim Mayo, clawing for a knife. Mayo caught the dogs, pulled himself erect, and then stuck out his foot. Demarest was thrown off balance and went to his knees, but then he was up. Ponga Jim jerked another of the dogs loose and spun around, bracing himself for Demarest's charge.

The man flung himself forward, and Mayo started a punch. It landed, but Demarest struck him in the chest with a shoulder. The door gave suddenly behind them, and both crashed through and fell, turning over and over, into the water!

Vaguely, Ponga Jim was grateful for the warmth of the water and then for its coolness. He felt someone clawing at him, pushed him away, and then caught hold and kept pushing. Darkness swam nearer through the water, and he lost consciousness once more.

When his eyes opened he stared up at a sort of net of steel, and when he tried to turn his head his neck was stiff as though he had taken a lot of punches. He tried to move, and someone said:

"Take it easy, mister."

He managed to get his head turned and saw a man in a British naval uniform standing by.

"What happened?" he asked.

"Everything's okay," the seaman said. "You're on the *Markland*, of Sydney. This is one of the convoy."

The seaman stuck his head out the door. "Tell the old man this guy is coming out of it," he yelled.

Almost at once a big, broad-shouldered man came through the door with a hand outstretched.

"Mayo!" he exclaimed. "Sink me for a lubber if I didn't get a start when they brought you over the side. You and that black man of yours!"

"What happened?" Ponga Jim asked. "How's the *Semiramis?*"

"Huh, you couldn't sink that old barge!" the captain roared. "Sure as my name's Brennan, you can't! But she's lost the starboard wing of her bridge, two guns are out of commission, there's a hole through the after deckhouse, and about ten feet of taffrail are blown away, but no men killed. Some shrapnel wounds. The sub got back safe."

The door pushed open, and Major Arnold came in.

"Hi, Jim!" He gripped Mayo's hand, grinning. "You did it again, darn you!"

"The *Khamsin?*"

"Still afloat, but the navy's after her. They are fighting a running battle toward Bab el Mandeb. But she's down by the head and badly hurt. She'll never get away. Everything else is under control. We got Theron. Your boys wiped out Mullens and his gang when they tried to get Kernan and me. Had them covered before they started to open fire, and killed them all with automatics at close range."

Arnold turned toward the door.

"General Kernan is here," he informed, "with Skelton. They want to see you. Skelton says he owes you an apology."

"Yeah?" Ponga Jim lifted himself on an elbow. "Listen, you—"

The door opened and General Kernan and Skelton came in. Skelton smiled.

"Fine work, Captain! We'll see you get a decoration for this."

Ponga Jim stared at him, his eyes cold. For an instant there was silence, and then Skelton's smile vanished, his eyes widened a little, and his muscles tensed.

"William," Ponga Jim said carefully, "arrest this man. He is a traitor. He was working hand in glove with Theron, and I have documentary evidence to prove it!"

"What?" Kernan roared. "Why, man, you're insane! You're—"

Skelton's eyes narrowed as he stared at Ponga Jim. Then he sprang back suddenly, and there was a gun in his hand.

"No," he said tightly, "he's right! If he says he has the evidence, I believe him. Theron told me someone stole some papers. Of course it's true! I've made fools of you all! And if it hadn't been for this thick-skulled sailor with his fool's luck, I'd have won, too! And so would Theron. He's a great man, Theron is, a great man! Do you hear?" His voice rose to a scream and then cut off sharply. "All right! But you three will die, anyway. You three—"

Big London's powerful black arm slipped through the door and around Skelton's throat. It tightened suddenly. The gun roared, and the bullet flattened against the bulkhead. Then London jerked, and there was an ominous crack. He dropped Skelton's body.

"I didn't mean for to kill him, Captain," he said. "But his neck was so little!"

"Who got me aboard here?" Jim said, ignoring the body.

Arnold swallowed. "Big London. He was coming behind in the small boat with two others as you had suggested when you said you'd unload as soon as possible. He dived in after you."

"Demarest?"

"Was that who you were fighting with?" Arnold frowned. "I had been watching him. I had the dope on him, but before I could have him arrested, he slipped away." He hesitated. "By the way, when we flew down to join the convoy and see how this end was going, we brought somebody with us. She wants to see you."

"She?"

"Yes."

Jim looked toward the voice. Zara Hammedan was standing in the door.

"Are you surprised?"

"Surprised?" Ponga Jim looked up at Arnold with a grin. "William, can't you see the lady wants to be alone with me?"

Arnold gave a snort and turned toward the door.

"And by the way, old chap," Ponga Jim added, "don't slam the door when you go out!"

"That guy!" Arnold said sarcastically. "Shoot him, drop him over the side, and he comes up with a blonde under one arm, and a brunette under the other! What can you do with a guy like that?"